CHRISTOPHER BUSH
THE CASE OF THE
DEADLY DIAMONDS

CHRISTOPHER BUSH was born Charlie Christmas Bush in Norfolk in 1885. His father was a farm labourer and his mother a milliner. In the early years of his childhood he lived with his aunt and uncle in London before returning to Norfolk aged seven, later winning a scholarship to Thetford Grammar School.

As an adult, Bush worked as a schoolmaster for 27 years, pausing only to fight in World War One, until retiring aged 46 in 1931 to be a full-time novelist. His first novel featuring the eccentric Ludovic Travers was published in 1926, and was followed by 62 additional Travers mysteries. These are all to be republished by Dean Street Press.

Christopher Bush fought again in World War Two, and was elected a member of the prestigious Detection Club.

He died in 1973.

CHRISTOPHER BUSH

THE CASE OF THE DEADLY DIAMONDS

With an introduction
by Curtis Evans

DEAN STREET PRESS

INTRODUCTION

> *Rosalind.* If it be true that good wine needs no bush [i.e., advertising], 'tis true that a good play needs no epilogue. Yet to good wine, they do use good bushes, and good plays prove the better by the help of good epilogues.
>
> —SHAKESPEARE, Epilogue, *As You Like It*

THE decade of the 1960s saw the sun finally begin to set on that storied generation which between the First and Second World Wars gave us detective fiction's Golden Age. Taking account of both deaths and retirements, by the late Sixties only a bare half-dozen pre-World War Two members of the Detection Club were still plying their deliciously deceptive craft: Agatha Christie, Anthony Gilbert (Lucy Beatrice Malleson), Gladys Mitchell, John Dickson Carr, Nicholas Blake and Christopher Bush, the subject of this introduction. Bush himself would pass away, at the age of eighty-seven, in 1973, having published, at the age of eighty-two, his sixty-third Ludovic Travers detective novel, *The Case of the Prodigal Daughter*, in the United Kingdom in the spring of 1968.

In the United States Bush's final detective novel did not appear until late November 1969, about four months after the horrific Manson murders in the tarnished Golden State of California. Implicating the triple terrors of sex, drugs and rock and roll (not to mention almost inconceivably bestial violence), the Manson slayings could not have strayed farther from the whimsically escapist "death as a game" aesthetic of Golden Age of detective fiction. Increasingly in the decade capable of producing psychedelic psychopaths like Charles Manson and his "family," the few remaining survivors of the Golden Age of detective fiction increasingly deemed themselves men and women far out of time. In his detective fiction John Dickson Carr, an incurable romantic, prudently beat a retreat from the present into the pleasanter pages of the past, setting his tales in bygone historical eras where he felt vastly more at home. With varying success Agatha Christie made a brave effort to stay abreast of the times (*Third Girl, Endless Night*), but ultimately her strivings to understand what was going on around her collapsed into the utter incoherence of *Passenger to Frankfurt* and *Postern of Fate*, by general consensus the worst mystery novels that Dame Agatha ever put down on paper.

In his detective fiction Christopher Bush, who was not quite two years older than Christie, managed rather better than the Queen of Crime to keep up with all the unsettling goings-on around him, while never forswearing the Golden Age article of faith that the primary purpose of a crime writer is pleasingly to puzzle his/her readers. And, in contrast with Christie and Carr, Bush knew when it was time to lay down his pen (or turn off his dictation machine, as the case may be), thereby allowing him to make his exit from the stage on a comparatively high note. Indeed, Christopher Bush's concluding baker's dozen of detective novels, which he published between 1957 and 1968 (and which have now been reprinted, after more than a half-century, by Dean Street Press), makes a generally fine epilogue, or coda, to the author's impressive corpus of crime fiction, which first began to see the light of day way back in the jubilant Jazz Age. These are, readers will find, "good bushes" (to punningly borrow from Shakespeare), providing them with ample intelligent detective entertainment as Bush's longtime series sleuth Ludovic Travers, in the luminous twilight of his career, makes his final forays into ingenious criminal investigation.

*

In the last thirteen Ludovic Travers mystery novels, Travers' *entrée* to his cases continues to come through his ownership of the Broad Street Detective Agency. Besides Travers we also regularly encounter his elegant wife, Bernice (although sometimes his independent-minded spouse is away on excursions of her own), his proverbially loyal secretary, Bertha Munney, his top Broad Street op, Hallows (another one named French, presumably inspired by Bush's late Detection Club colleague Freeman Wills Crofts, pops up occasionally), John Hill of the United Assurance Agency, who brings Travers many of his cases, and Scotland Yard's Inspector Jewle and Sergeant Matthews, who after the first of these final novels, *The Case of the Treble Twist* (in the U. S. *Triple Twist*), are promoted, respectively, to Superintendent and Inspector. (The Yard's ex-Superintendent George Wharton, now firmly retired from any form of investigative work whatsoever, is mentioned just once by Ludo, when, in *The Case of the Dead Man Gone*, he passingly imparts that he and Wharton recently had lunch together.)

For all practical purposes Travers, who during the Golden Age was a classic gentleman amateur snooper like Philo Vance and Lord Peter Wimsey, now functions fully as a professional private eye—although one, to be sure, who is rather posher than the rest. While some reviewers referred to Travers as England's Philip Marlowe, in fact he little resembles the general run of love and leave 'em/hate and beat 'em brand of brutish American P. I.'s, favoring a nice cup of coffee (a post-war change from tea), a good pipe and the occasional spot of sherry to the frequent snatches of liquor and cigarettes favored by most of his American brethren and remaining faithful to his spouse despite encountering a succession of sexy women, not all of them, shall we say, virtuously inclined.

This was a formula which throughout the period maintained a devoted audience on both sides of the Atlantic consisting, one surmises, of readers (including crime writers Anthony Berkeley, Nicholas Blake and the late Alan Hunter, creator of Inspector George Gently) who preferred their detectives something less than hardboiled. Travers himself sneers at the hugely popular (and psychotically violent) postwar American private eye Mike Hammer, commenting of an American couple in *The Case of the Treble Twist*: "She was a woman of considerable culture; his ran about as far as Mickey Spillane" [a withering reference to Mike Hammer's creator]. Yet despite his manifest disdain for Mike Hammer, an ugly American if ever there were one, Christopher Bush and his wife Florence in the spring of 1957 had traveled to New York aboard the RMS *Queen Elizabeth*, and references by him to both the United States and Canada became more frequent in the books which followed this trip.

Certainly *The Case of the Treble Twist* (1957) features tough customers and an exceptionally cruel murder, yet it is also one of Bush's most ingeniously contrived cases from the Fifties, full of charm, treacherous deception and, yes, plenty of twists, including one that is a real sockaroo (to borrow, as Bush occasionally did, from

American idiom). Similarly clever is *The Case of the Running Man* (1958), which draws, as several earlier Bush books had, on the author's profound love and knowledge of antiques. By this time Bush and his wife, their coffers having burgeoned from the proceeds of his successful mysteries, resided in the quaint medieval market town of Lavenham, Suffolk at the Great House, a splendidly decorated fourteenth-century structure with an elegant Georgian-era façade which he and Florence purchased in 1953 and resided in until their deaths. The dashing author, whom in 1967 *Chicago Tribune* mystery reviewer Alice Crombie swooningly dubbed "one of the handsomest mystery writers on either side of the Channel or Atlantic," also drove a Jaguar, beloved by James Bond films of late, well into his eighties.

The Case of the Running Man includes that Golden Age detective fiction staple, a family tree, but more originally the novel features as a major character a black American man, Sam, the devoted chauffeur of the wealthy murder victim. Sam, who reminds Ludovic Travers of Rochester, "Jack Benny's factotum of television and radio," is an interesting and sincerely treated individual, although as Anthony Boucher amusingly pronounced at the time in the *New York Times Book Review*, he speaks "a dialect never heard by mortal ear"—an odd compounding of "American Negro" and London cockney.

The Case of the Careless Thief (1959) takes Ludo to Sandbeach, "the Blackpool of the South Coast," as the American jacket blurb puts it, with "a dozen hotels, a race track, a dog track, a music hall and two enormous dance halls." Anthony Boucher deemed this hard-hitting, tricky tale, which draws to strong effect on contemporary events in England, "one of Ludovic Travers' best cases." Likewise hard-hitting are *The Case of the Sapphire Brooch* (1960) and *The Case of the Extra Grave* (1961), complex tales of murderous mésalliances with memorably grim conclusions. The plot of *The Case of the Dead Man Gone* (1961) topically involves refugee relief groups, while *The Case of the Heavenly Twin* (1963) opens with a case of a creative criminal couple forging American Express Travelers Checks, concerning which Americans of a certain age will recall actor Karl Malden sternly enjoining, in a long-running television advertising campaign: "Don't leave home without them." In contrast with many of his crime writing contemporaries (judging from the tone of their work), Bush actually learned to watch and enjoy television, although in *The Case of Three-Ring Puzzle*, a tale of violently escalating intrigue, Travers dryly references Scottish philosopher Thomas Carlyle's famous observation that England's population consisted of "mostly fools" when he comments: "I guess he wasn't too far out at that. But rather remarkable an estimate perhaps, considering that in his day there were no television commercials."

Of Bush's final five Ludovic Travers detective novels, published between 1964 and 1968, when the Western World, in the eyes of many, was going from whimsically mod to utterly mad, the best are, in my estimation, the cases of *The Jumbo Sandwich* (1965), *The Good Employer* (1966) and *The Prodigal Daughter* (1968). In *Sandwich* a crisp case of a defrauded (and jilted) gentry lady friend of Ludo's metamorphoses into a smorgasbord of, as the American book jacket puts it, "blackmail, black magic, a black sheep, and murder." It all culminates in a confrontation on a lonely Riviera beach in France, setting of some of Ludovic Travers' earliest cases, between Ludo and a desperate killer, in which Bernice plays an unexpectedly active part. Ludo again travels to France in the highly classic *Employer*, which draws most engagingly on the sleuth's (and the author's) dabbling in the world of art and is dedicated to his distinguished Lavenham artist friends, the couple Reginald and Rosalie Brill, who resided next door to Bush and his wife at the fourteenth-century Little Hall, then an art student hostel for which the Brills served as guardians. In *The Guardian* Francis Iles (aka Golden Age crime writer Anthony Berkeley) pronounced that *Employer* represented Bush "at his most ingenious."

Finally, in *Daughter* Travers finds himself tasked with recovering the absconded teenage offspring of domineering Dora Marport, sober-sided head of the organization Home and Family, which is righteously devoted to "the fostering, so to speak, of family life as the stoutest bulwark against the encroachment of ever-more numerous hostile forces: sex and violence in literature, films and on television; pornography generally, and the erosion of responsibility and the capability for sacrifice by the welfare state." Can Travers, a Great War veteran who made his debut in detective fiction in 1926, bridge the generation gap in late-Sixties London? Ludo may prefer Bach to the Beatles, but in this, the last of his recorded cases, he proves more "with it" than one might have expected. All in All, *Daughter* makes a rewarding finish to one of the longest-running and most noteworthy sleuth series in British detective fiction.

Curtis Evans

PART I: CRIME AND PUNISHMENT

1. TWO HUNDRED POUNDS

IT WAS on a Tuesday morning of early November, 1961, that Vigors rang me and asked if he could slip along to see me. He said he wouldn't keep me more than a few minutes. I said I was perfectly free and I'd be glad to see him.

We at the Broad Street Detective Agency do a great deal of work for United Assurance, and Vigors is one of their principal claims inspectors. Bob Hallows, my fellow director, is usually the one to handle that side of the business, but he was away up north engaged on another job, so, whatever it was that Vigors had in mind, it looked as if I'd be the one to take over. It mightn't, of course, be anything of great consequence: indeed, if it had been, then John Hill, the managing director, would almost certainly have rung me direct. My guess happened to be right. Almost the first thing Vigors said was that he was acting entirely on his own responsibility in what might be something easily explicable.

"But it's something that's worrying you?"

"It is," he said. "The claim's for only two hundred pounds and from a client who's insured with us far more importantly, and yet there's something peculiar about it. It's a matter of a burglary, or a theft, and yet the client doesn't want it reported to the police."

"You think it might be an inside job and he's trying a roundabout way of hushing it up?"

"Could be," he said. "Perhaps I'd better tell you the whole thing."

It turned out that the client was a Karl Morren of The Elms, Cockfosters: a manufacturing jeweller and valuer. He held the usual fire and burglary policy on the house. Early the previous day—the Monday morning—he'd reported that approximately two hundred pounds in cash was missing from a wall safe in his house. It had actually been placed there on the previous Saturday morning. His local bank would confirm that he had cashed a cheque for that amount. It had been his custom to have that amount of money in the house at the beginning of a month so as to meet household expenses which would include the wages of a married couple—cook-general and gardener-handyman. He had actually discovered on the Sunday evening that the money was missing, and the next morning had decided to report to the insurance company.

"I rang him up before I rang you," Vigors said, "and asked him what the police were doing. He said he hadn't informed them. When I asked why not, he did some shilly-shallying, or so it seemed to me. Said the matter wasn't important enough. Also that he'd looked round himself and couldn't find any signs of entry. I put to him what you put to me, that it might be an inside job, and he was most indignant. Only himself and his wife and the married couple were in the house that Saturday night, and the couple could be implicitly trusted. So that was that. Naturally I had to handle him carefully, but I did ask if anything else had been taken. He said not a thing as far as he'd been able to check."

"And then?"

"Well, I still meant to handle him carefully, so I said he wasn't to have any doubts about the claim being met, but we would esteem it a favour if one of our people could have a quick look round and would he suggest a time. He suggested five o'clock this evening and I said we'd be there."

"We being you and I?"

"That's what I hoped."

"Don't see why not," I said. "Four o'clock at Lombard Street suit you?"

He said he'd be ready for me, and got up to go.

"Just a minute, if you're not in too much of a hurry. Tell me a bit more about the client, this Karl Morren. The name doesn't sound too English."

"It is and it isn't," he said. "The father came from Amsterdam and became naturalised. His wife was actually English. She died just before him and he died some four years ago, and the son, Karl, took over the business which his father had founded. He's getting on for fifty, and he's been in it all his life in any case."

"And the business actually is what?"

"I think I told you," he said. "He's a manufacturing jeweller and valuer."

I think I frowned.

"You mean he manufactures jewellery, just like that? Costume jewellery?"

He smiled. "Nothing like that. He carries out special commissions from very high-class firms indeed, either to their designs or he submits his own. The finished article might run into quite a big sum of money. Things like large-carat, good-quality diamonds, for instance, come pretty dear. Emeralds, carat for carat, even dearer. Also there's gold and platinum."

"Where's his business premises?"

People like Vigors have to have good memories. He didn't consult any notes.

"In Corby Street, Clerkenwell. Quite an unpretentious place. Only three people there besides himself."

"All the same, he must be pretty heavily insured."

"Just a matter of comparison, but it isn't inconsiderable. He never carries more stock than he's handling at any given moment, and that's automatically insured."

"And his wife. Know anything about her?"

"Nothing, except that we hold a life insurance for only a moderate sum."

"No children?"

"Two," he said. "There were life insurances on both for quite small amounts, but the son came of age about a year ago and that policy lapsed. The daughter, Greta, is still well under age."

I didn't detain him for more than another minute, and when he'd gone I didn't sit brooding over the case any longer than it took me to drink my usual morning cup of coffee. After that I had nothing whatever on hand, and it was chiefly the desire to kill time that made me walk through to Clerkenwell. What I hoped to find there I didn't know. If it was the hope that it could be something that might throw light on the burglary, then that hope was a flagrant self-deception.

Corby Street isn't all that far from Broad Street, and it didn't take long to find the Morren premises at No. 72. It was, indeed, an unpretentious place: twin-curtained windows and a door, and the frontage about thirty feet.

Over the door was K. MORREN. IMPORT AGENT. The paintwork looked reasonably new. It probably dated from the four years ago when the father had died and the name had had to be altered.

Corby Street itself could be called a third-rate shopping area. On one side of the Morren place was a photographer's and a second-hand furniture shop on the other. Farther down the street were some kerbside stalls and quite a few people were about. Morren's, I told myself, was pretty well camouflaged for a business which could very well have been just off or even in Bond Street.

I wondered if there were a back entry, so I walked on as far as the first of the stalls and took a left-hand turn into Hanbury Terrace. It was a residential area, and so was the first on the left again. I went quite a way along till it was obvious that there was no back way to the Morren premises, except, of course, through someone else's house and back garden. After that I made a meandering way back to Broad Street, and, honest for once with myself, I knew that all I'd done was to get Broad Street out of my system for an idle hour and cast a contemplative eye on a part of the city that I knew none too well. While that didn't exactly make me the Marco Polo of the age, it did at least bring me to within a few minutes of lunch. The last thing that might have occurred to me as I was eating it in my usual pub was that in the reasonably near future I should be seeing Corby Street again.

From Cockfosters Station it was about five minutes' walk. All that once pleasant country area had changed enormously since I'd last seen it. Houses had sprung up everywhere, and quite a few, like The Elms, well above the ten-thousand pound class. I don't know why, but I was a bit taken aback at the first sight of it.

The house was architect-built with a double garage at the near end as we approached. A storey above the garage was probably the living quarters of the married couple who comprised the staff. The house itself was brick-built in a Georgian style, with a circular drive that led in and out. How many rooms there were we couldn't guess, but there must have been at least half a dozen bedrooms. The gardens ran well back, with summer shade from the two huge elms that gave the house its name.

The near half of the garage was open, and through it we could see a green Jaguar.

"Quite a smell of money," I said to Vigors. "Morren must be doing well."

"Maybe. This was probably bought, though, from the father's estate."

A pleasant-faced, middle-aged woman answered our ring. She ushered us into quite a large hall and took our hats and overcoats. A door opened and through it we could see the lounge as another woman appeared.

"Oh!" she said, as if surprised. "You must be the people to see my husband. I'm Beryl Morren."

There were introductions. She spoke to the woman, whose name was May. Would she tell the master his visitors had arrived. He'd probably be in the greenhouse. And would she see the garage closed. She'd forgotten to lock it when she'd brought in her car.

"Shall we go in?" she asked us sweetly. "And I'm sure you'd like tea."

Vigors told her we'd had an early tea in town. I was running an eye over that large but very comfortable lounge. There wasn't much in the antique line to interest me except a couple of chests—probably Dutch—that flanked an early eighteenth-century lacquered clock by the far wall.

Beryl Morren herself was far more interesting. She was tall—about five-nine—and with the figure of a woman in the twenties, and at that age she must have been uncommonly handsome.

The complexion, or the make-up, was still perfect, but the face had a definite hardness. I didn't know whether or not it was some kind of affectation, but the mouth had every now and again an expression of tolerant amusement: the kind one assumes, maybe, when trying to be pleasant with one's social inferiors. Everything about her looked expensive. Little as I know about women's clothes, I guessed the afternoon frock she was wearing must have cost a packet, and there was nothing phoney about her earrings and the three-stone ring.

Vigors and I were on the beautifully sprung settee before the open fire. She faced us from a matching chintz-covered chair.

"You're here to see us about the missing money," she began.

Vigors said that was so. She leaned confidentially forward.

"Don't you think Karl—my husband—takes things a bit too seriously? A storm in a tea-cup, wouldn't you call it?"

"Maybe it's a matter of principle," Vigors told her. "Even a claim of two hundred pounds has to have some scrutiny. Five pounds, five thousand pounds, it's all the same. In this case, of course, it's largely formal."

"That's what I mean," she told him triumphantly. "To a company like yours, what's two hundred pounds? Surely Karl must have exaggerated."

The far door opened and Morren came in. He looked rather older than what I was to learn was his forty-seven years, though the blond hair showed no trace of grey. He was about six feet, and spare. He was clean-shaven and the cheeks slightly sunken. It was to me that he held out his hand.

"Mr. Vigors?"

I explained, and finally we all sat down: he in a chair near his wife, and facing us.

"Right," he said. "Let's talk this deplorable business over. Perhaps you'd excuse us for a bit, Beryl."

"But I want to hear it," she told him amusedly. "After all, I'm concerned as much as you."

"Very well." The tone was a bit curt. "Perhaps you'll give us your ideas, Mr. Vigors."

Vigors began with a suave apology. What he had to say and the questions he had to ask were largely routine. Certain things were laid down and written into policies and it was his job—sometimes an unpleasant one—to act according to the rules.

"In this case, of course, it's more routine than ever. There'll be no difficulty about meeting the claim. But just for our records, Mr. Morren, would you be so good as to go over the whole thing quickly again?"

I might have been deceived, but Morren looked a bit relieved. He said he rarely went to the city on a Saturday but spent an hour or two in the garden and did various chores, if, of course, he weren't away on some valuation. At eleven o'clock he'd cashed the cheque at the bank and had come straight back and put the notes in the safe. Of course we could see the safe.

It was in the dining-room. We entered it through a door at the far left of the lounge. More old Dutch furniture here, and behind a mediocre Dutch landscape the safe itself, a tiny affair of twelve by nine. It opened with a key.

"Yours is the only key?"

"No," he said. "My wife has to have one. I keep mine on this chain with the spare car keys and the front-door key."

"Mind if Mr. Travers has a look?"

I put my glass on the lock. There was never a sign of scratching. Bob Hallows could have opened that lock inside ten seconds, but even he would have left some sort of trace.

"And the key never left your possession?"

"Of course not."

"Don't be ridiculous, Karl." I wasn't even aware she'd followed us in. "You're always leaving things lying about. Only last week we had to search the house for those keys, and where should they be but in the breakfast-room."

"That was once in a lifetime," he told her annoyedly.

"And your own key, Mrs. Morren?"

"Always in my bag."

Vigors wanted to know about door keys. They were comparatively simple. The married couple had a key to the side or tradesmen's door. The Morrens had keys to the front door and the breakfast-room: a south-facing room that had french windows opening on the back lawn.

"Could we see it?"

It was a pleasant-looking room facing due south: a sun-trap for practically all the year. Through the windows we could see almost nothing, for dusk had long since fallen and there was a trace of mist in the air. I used my small torch and glass and examined the lock. There seemed nothing abnormal. I asked if there were any other keys.

"Only one which my daughter has," Morren said. "She's working with a firm of couturiers in town and often has to stay late, and if she decides to come home she uses this door so as not to disturb the house. Also—you know what young people are these days—most of her interests are in town: dancing, I imagine, and that kind of thing; so if she's very late she stays with my son. He has quite a large apartment in Flagon Street. You know it?"

"Just off Regent Street?"

"That's right," he said. "He did very well at Cambridge, and when he came down he wanted to go into publishing. He's with London Publications in Handel Street and doing quite well. We were lucky to find him this apartment in Flagon Street. That's quite near. My wife and I furnished it for him."

We went back to the lounge. Morren offered us a drink and we accepted, and over it the talk was quite pleasant. If there was one discordant sound, it came from Vigors just before we rose to go.

"Well, that's probably the last you'll hear of this business," Vigors said. "Except for just one thing. If you read through your policy again, Mr. Morren, you'll see that it was incumbent on you to notify the police. It follows that nothing should have been touched till after their inspection. But you must definitely inform them now. We'll receive their report within two or three days, after which you'll receive our cheque."

Beryl Morren wanted to know if that were really necessary. Vigors patiently went over it again.

"For heaven's sake. Beryl, let it rest," Morren told her exasperatedly. "The sooner the whole thing's settled, the sooner we can have some peace and quiet for once." He got to his feet. "Sorry about this, but the whole business has been very disturbing."

We assured him we understood. A few more soothing words, thanks for the drinks and for the promised co-operation, and we were being shown out. Morren offered to drive us back to the station. We thanked him but declined.

"Well, what do you make of it all?" Vigors asked me.

I said frankly that I didn't know. All I had at the moment were certain impressions.

"Such as?"

"One is that money doesn't make a happy household. I'd call that one a most unhappy one."

"Yes," he said. "I'd say Morren has a very expensive wife. Maybe that's what's worrying him. You thought he was worried?"

"If he isn't, a man doesn't snap at his wife in front of strangers. Not that she didn't give him cause. Deliberate cause. By the way, is there anything else you know about him? His reputation, for instance?"

"It's a very good reputation. He's one of the very best authorities on jewellery, antique and modern."

"Business good?"

"I imagine so. His work's absolutely first-class. He can afford to pick and choose."

"All the same, he has some pretty big overheads, and not only as affecting the firm itself. Has the wife any money?"

"Don't know," he said. "I might find out."

"Even if she has, there's the upkeep of that house. Staff, rates and taxes and so on. There's a daughter of about eighteen who presumably still has to be helped, and the son was at Cambridge. He mayn't yet be standing on his own feet either. Did you notice any difference, by the way, in how he spoke of his children. I thought there was a definite affection in how he spoke of his son and a disappointment in the daughter."

"I agree," he said. "But young people these days want to live their own lives, and pretty hectic lives they can be. By our standards, I mean. I know. I have a son of eighteen and a daughter sixteen. If I didn't tell myself they were—well, fundamentally sound—I'd be badly worried."

We didn't do any talking on the train, but when we were walking towards Lombard Street he wanted to know what my opinions were: strictly, of course, in confidence. I hesitated for a moment.

"I'll make you a bet," I finally said. "A couple of lunches that the police find no signs whatever of entry."

"Agreed," he said. "I owe you a lunch in any case. I can't very well charge you up to the firm."

"Forget it," I told him. "Some day I'll ask you for a favour. But you didn't ask me what actually happened. Or would you like to give me your own ideas: still strictly in confidence."

"Well, I think the wife simply helped herself to the money and hoped for the best. You disagree?"

"Not at all," I said. "That was my idea after I'd been no more than a few minutes inside the house."

*

Vigors said he'd keep me informed, and he did. Three days later he told me he'd had the confidential report from the police. They'd found no trace whatever of a forced entry. In their opinion it had to be an inside job.

Early the following week he told me the claim had been settled. One other piece of information. Beryl Morren, as far as could be ascertained, had no private means. When Morren married her she had been a receptionist in a high-class West End hotel.

A day or two later he insisted on my lunching with him. We're both in the same line of business—investigation—so it was natural that we should talk shop, even if the Morren business was not only a thing of the past but most unlikely to be reopened whatever we or the police might happen to discover.

That it had been an inside job we were both sure. That Beryl had helped herself to the two hundred pounds we were now not so sure. After all, she had a key to that safe and was known, and entitled, to have it. Also she was very far from a fool. Suspicion was bound to fall on herself, and she couldn't have helped but know it.

Could Morren have taken it himself, hoping that suspicion would fall on his wife? Did the antagonism we suspected existed between them extend to anything so rather horrible as that? We doubted it. In a way it would have been childish. And what could it have led to that couldn't have been achieved by simpler means?

No. As far as Morren was concerned, everything was what he had made it out to be. On the Saturday morning he had put the money in the safe, and when he had expected to find it there on the Sunday evening it had gone.

"Why the Sunday evening? Seems a queer time. Why not the Monday morning? After all, you don't need household money on Sunday? Or do you?"

"Ah," Vigors said. "I can explain that. It was in the confidential report we had from the police. They went into things quite deeply. First of all, they were pretty sure the domestic staff had nothing to do with it. That left the son and the daughter. Now the daughter wasn't at home at all on the Saturday. She and her brother joined a man named Sievers for dinner and dancing at a West End hotel. They left around midnight and then Sievers went home to Northwood and the other two went to the brother's apartment."

"Know anything else about this Sievers?"

"Only that he's Frank Sievers. You must have seen one of their jewellers' shops in town. There's one at Holborn."

I said I remembered the one in Cheapside. But what was the connection between Sievers and the Morren children? Vigors had gathered there was some sort of understanding between this Frank Sievers and Greta Morren, and the brother was a kind of chaperone.

"And the Sunday?"

"Well, the children arrived at Cockfosters at about noon. The son nearly always spent the Sunday with his parents in any case. Nothing happened till after the evening meal when the son was going back to town and he remembered that his father had promised to pay a small repair bill. Morren hadn't enough money in his wallet so he went to the safe. Beryl Morren had to give her son the money: only a matter of twelve pounds odd."

"And the family reactions?"

Vigors only knew what the police had been told: that no one could believe it. The upshot was that Morren said he was going to sleep on it before deciding what action to take.

"One other thing. It won't surprise you, but the Morrens occupy separate bedrooms."

I said he was right. It didn't surprise me at all.

2. THE DIAMONDS

WE DON'T run the agency in watertight compartments. Norris—a kind of works manager—looks after accounts and helps assign operatives; Bob Hallows does chiefly insurance work, and I do what private work happens to be going. But that apparently strict set-up doesn't preclude co-operation and a sort of interdependence. So when Hallows got back from his trip up north I gave him an account of the Morren affair.

Almost exactly two months later, one day early in January, he came back to the agency after lunch and pushed an early evening paper under my nose, thumb on a paragraph.

"This interest you?"

I had a look at it.

BURGLARY IN CLERKENWELL

Police were called last night to the premises of K. Morren in Corby Street, Clerkenwell, where it had been reported that something suspicious was taking place. It is understood that a man is now helping the police with their enquiries.

I'd be exaggerating if I said I was surprised. At that moment it was only a coincidence. I'd known Morren, and now there'd been a burglary at his business premises, and that was all. Still, neither Hallows nor I had anything particular on hand, so we began talking about that old Morren affair. I hadn't mentioned to him that I'd actually seen the Corby Street place, so I told him about it: how unobtrusive it was and how the jewellery manufacturing appeared on the sign above the door as an import business.

"You know anything about jewellery manufacturing?" I asked him.

In the course of years I've accumulated a lot of facts, but chiefly about what one might call the esoteric: the kind of accreted information that makes the solving of crosswords comparatively easy. I'm not trying to be clever when I say that Hallows doesn't suffer from the handicap of a public school and a university. He's been in the detection business from the time he left his school. He knows the city like his own back garden, he has sources of information which never cease to amaze me, and he has a prodigious memory. Even then I hardly expected him to know a great deal about the jewellery manufacturing business. I was wrong.

He sort of frowned for a moment or two and then said the trade might come under three headings. In Birmingham, for instance, there were hundreds of small firms—father-and-son affairs—that made jewellery to the specifications of whomever employed them. It might range from costume jewellery to the stuff sold over the counter in jewellers' shops.

Then there were the free-lance designers of more valuable stuff who had connections in the high-grade world. They knew the fashion trends and the latest processes. It was their job to do so. Finally, there were the really big firms like Carringtons who employed their own design staff.

"And Morren—where does he fit in?"

"Apparently he's a man with a high reputation. As a valuer he'd see interesting things, old and new. He'd be listened to when he put ideas to the big firms. He could submit designs or agree to work on theirs."

It seemed clear enough to me. "And he'd have got his knowledge from working with his father?"

"Not till later. That'd be my guess. He probably went to a School of Arts and Crafts—like the one in Southampton Row. They'd teach him manipulation of metals and stones, design and what you might call the tradesman's side of it. When he went into his father's business he'd be equipped with a first-class foundation."

When I asked him with something of awe how he came to know so much about it, he said it was easy. His own son-in-law was a designer for one of the big firms, and he'd been through the same hoop. I couldn't help laughing.

At around four-thirty that same afternoon we were discussing over a cup of tea some business in Norris's office when Bertha Munney, our secretary-receptionist, put through a call.

"Yes, he's here," Norris said, and whispered "John Hill" as he handed over the receiver.

"Travers here," I said.

"This is John Hill. Could you see me?"

"When?"

"Straight away, if possible. Hallows there too? If so, I'd like to see both of you."

I told him we'd be at Lombard Street in about ten minutes. United Assurance is easily our best client, and when Hill whistles we run.

We weren't more than a minute or two late. Hill wasn't in his desk chair: he was standing ruminatively, arms behind him, with his back to the handsome electric fire. He asked if we'd like tea or a drink. Since his call had ruined the tea we should have had, I said tea sounded pretty good.

He went across to his desk and we got ourselves seated.

"Sorry to be so urgent," he said, "but we look like taking a bit of a knock. Just over ten thousand pounds. A burglary in Clerkenwell."

"Wasn't there something in the evening papers about it?" I said.

"If it was to do with a firm called K. Morren, it was," he said. "But I wouldn't have called you in for that. Not both of you. After all, the claim isn't all that large. It has various peculiar circumstances that I don't like."

The tea was brought in and we helped ourselves. I took a sip of mine and asked him what the peculiar circumstances were. He smiled a bit wryly.

"There're so many I hardly know where to begin."

He glanced at some notes and I did some quick thinking. In a huge organisation like United Assurance responsibilities must be absolute. Hill would know nothing of so comparatively trivial an affair as the theft of £200 at the Morren home. Ought I to be ignorant too?

Would it be wise to mention Vigors? For the moment I didn't know. But we both sat quiet while Hill told us about the K. Morren firm. Only one previous claim in nearly thirty years, and that a small one. And now this, completely out of the blue.

He said he'd been in touch with the Yard and was in possession of information, most of which wouldn't be released. The burglary had taken place the previous night, but the police had been given a tip-off. The burglar had been caught after quite a chase in the actual premises by the officers of a couple of squad cars. He had refused to talk and hadn't yet been identified.

"Perhaps you'd like to take some notes while I start at the actual beginning," he said. "Lorenz Brander is a diamond dealer of repute from Amsterdam, and he also happens to be Karl Morren's first cousin. He brings in stones occasionally under the usual licence, and as Morren wanted diamonds for a big job he was about to handle, Brander came over. Brander also intended to kill two birds with one stone by seeing old friends and also some clients in Birmingham. At any rate, he saw Morren at Corby Street at about five yesterday afternoon, and Morren purchased stones to the value of just over ten thousand pounds. Don't look surprised. Everything's relative. A single stone can easily be worth that much. What Morren bought was a mixed bag.

"The diamonds were put in the safe. It's the finest of its kind—Walters and Brown—and then the place was left in charge of Morren's head man and the two went to Brander's hotel—the Eversleigh in Norton Street. At half-past six they were joined by Morren's son and daughter. Mrs. Morren would have been there but for a previous engagement. They had dinner and then sat and talked in one of the lounges till around nine o'clock. The son went to his apartment, the daughter went home with her father, and Brander went to bed early because he wanted to be up early. That's Morren's account of things as it was passed on to me."

Hallows wanted to ask a question. "Do we take it that Brander's visits were sort of family affairs?"

"Yes," Hill said. "In a way. He really regarded his trips over here as more in the nature of holidays. Seeing relatives and old friends and doing a little business on the side. He's Morren's first cousin, as I think I said. And his only living relative. Hence the family gathering at the hotel."

I wanted to hear about the actual burglary, but Hill knew little more than he'd already told us. What we didn't know were the peculiar circumstances he'd said were puzzling him.

"There's the matter of inside knowledge," he said. "Was it a speculative job or did the burglar know the diamonds'd be there? Then there's the fact that the safe was open. It wasn't blown: just open. So how did he get the combination?"

"That makes it an inside job?"

Hill shrugged his shoulders.

"That's what the police'll try to find out. But there's something else. Where're the diamonds? The thief didn't have them on him. If he secreted them after being alarmed, then I gather the whole place has been gone over and not a trace. Superintendent Jewle hinted at a confederate."

It looked to me as if the place to start investigations was Corby Street. Hallows thought we might do better if we managed to see Jewle. I thought he was right. Hill, in any case, had no more to tell us. But he did ring Jewle.

It was the rush hour, but we managed to squeeze ourselves into a Tube train. From Charing Cross we walked, and talked.

Jewle was a very old friend, and that, we hoped, should make things easy. The burglar had been caught, and when he talked Jewle's job would be practically done. If there'd been confederates, then Jewle would still be interested, and no enquiries along those lines could possibly be a conflict of interests. All we wanted was the diamonds. If Jewle got them, well and good. If in the course of looking for them we came across facts that would interest Jewle, we'd be only too happy to pass them on. It looked a perfect set-up.

"Except for one thing," Hallows said. "If the burglar's talked, then Jewle either has the diamonds already or will have in a couple of shakes. That leaves us without a job. And the probable reward."

Jewle was alone in his room. As I've said, he's a very old friend. One way and another, we've worked together for years, and worked harmoniously too, even when a case itself meant drawing some remarkably fine lines. But this case, as he agreed, seemed far from complex. There was no quarrel between what he wanted and what we were after ourselves—ten thousand pounds' worth of diamonds in the usual small velvet bag.

"Can't help you yet," he said. "The prisoner still won't talk, and he's the only one who knows."

"What's he like?"

"Not the old type. About thirty or under, well-dressed, good-looking. No record."

I smiled. "Not a latter-day Raffles?"

"He looks the part," he said. "I'm pretty sure he's an amateur. And operating with a partner."

"You'll send out a picture?"

"There'll be one on television tonight," he said. "Before the night's out we ought to know who he is."

"And why are you so sure about a partner? You mean the one from whom he got the combination of the safe?"

"That we haven't yet cleared up," he said. "I'm talking about the one who's probably got the stones."

I stared.

"Tell you what," he said. "Meet me tomorrow morning—nine o'clock, say—and see the layout. Meanwhile here's an account of what happened, just for you two to think over. There was a 999 tip-off at a few minutes before six. A woman's voice, slightly Cockney, saying the place was going to be robbed. Two squad cars were sent, but it was a very misty night. One stopped short and the other beyond. The men from one car explored the streets behind and got permission to be in the back garden of the house immediately behind the Morren premises. It wasn't too promising for a getaway because the small back yard of the premises has an eight-foot wall round it with broken glass on top.

"The mist was patchy—almost a fog—but a movement was seen at the front door of the premises. The men waited a minute, then moved in. The front door was shut but they manipulated the Yale lock and went inside. There was a faint noise from upstairs, so one stayed at the foot and the other went up. The door at the head of the stairs—the one to Morren's office—was locked from inside, so he called his mate and they shouldered it open. The door into the next room had to be opened too, and by that time their man had dropped from the window to the yard and had cut his hand trying to get over the wall. He caved in without any fight. Meanwhile, we think his partner had slipped the yard or two along the passage and down the stairs and out at the front. Remember the diamonds were definitely there and they'd gone. Our man hadn't them on him, and we can swear they aren't on the premises or weren't thrown over the wall."

Hallows wanted to know something. Could the partner have been a safe expert? There for the express purpose of opening the safe?

Jewle didn't think even the best man in the business could have opened it in time—by sound and touch, that is. There was just the chance, of course, that he'd got in first. The tip-off had said the job would be done between six and half-past and it was ten-past when the cars got there.

"Leave it till the morning," Jewle advised us. "Nothing like seeing things on the spot. If anything happens before then I'll see that you're informed."

The first thing I did when I got home was to get hold of Vigors. Lombard Street gave me his private number. I put him in the picture and left it to him to decide whether or not there might be a remote connection between this latest case and the affair we'd both been engaged on in November. He thanked me and said he'd probably bring it to Hill's notice.

Mind you, I saw the glimmerings of a connection. No more than that. It wasn't even based on known facts. You could hardly call it even a hunch, and yet it seemed to me that something was there. It was this. A safe had been opened at Morren's house by someone with a knowledge of what was in it. A safe had been opened at Corby Street with a *possible*—I stress that word possible—knowledge of what was in it. There was also another question which in itself was a kind of connecting link. How had the Corby Street safe been opened? Had it been the simple matter of knowing the combination? And if so, from where had the knowledge been obtained?

After the evening meal Bernice—my wife—and I watched television. It was one of the better nights, but I was really waiting for the news and the picture of a man to be thrown on the screen. It came at the very end of the news. It was the face of a man in probably the late twenties; a good-looking, almost patrician face. I took the details down. Slim, athletic build, height five-ten, hair and eyes brown, a tattooed figure of a boxer just above the right wrist.

Soon after ten Bernice went to bed. I sat on, hoping for more news. It came at about half-past ten.

"That Mr. Ludovic Travers?"

"Speaking."

"Confidential message for you, sir, from Chief Superintendent Jewle. You ready to receive?"

I said I was.

"Then the man concerned is a David Wayner, aged twenty-seven. Last known address—The Carlo, Chester Street, Finsbury Park. Message ends. Shall I repeat?"

He repeated, I thanked him and rang off. Then I rang Hallows.

"Conveys little to me either," he said. "I do know The Carlo, though. It was one of those old monstrosities of skating rinks. Harry Alders bought it about four years ago. You remember him?"

"If so, it's only vaguely."

"He was welterweight champion twenty years ago. One of the few who hung on to his money. Went into promoting and had a boxer or two of his own. Owns a betting shop or two as well."

"What's The Carlo now?"

"Everything. Ten-pin bowling alley, basement restaurant and a first-class gym on the first floor. I gather it's another of Harry's goldmines."

"His nose is clean?"

"Clean as they come," he said. "I know him. Had business with him years ago before you bought the agency. Funny thing about this David Wayner, though. Something's been telling me I've heard of him before, and damned if I can think where."

"It'll come," I said. "See you in the morning at Corby Street. Maybe you'll have thought of it then."

3. AT CORBY STREET

WHAT a difference a little sun can make! The November morning when I'd last seen Corby Street had been dull with a threat of rain. Now it was sunny: cold but clear, and the street itself somehow brought sharply into focus. Everything 28 seemed more lively: the early traffic, the "Hurry along, please!" of the bus conductor and the flurry of sparrows disturbed by a passing car. In some queer way it was a more friendly street. It was no longer incongruous that Morren should have his business there.

I supposed it must have been some type of snobbishness that had almost instinctively made me think, with something of horror, that a firm which handled precious metals and stones should choose to work in an area which, on that drab November morning, had looked almost squalid. The folly was all the greater since there was something romantic in the very name of Clerkenwell—the holy well where once the clerks of London used to perform miracle plays. More mundane and very much more to the point was the fact that that part of Finsbury had almost always been a centre for jewellers and watch and clock makers. In fact, the Morren who had founded the firm had opened it in just the right place.

Bob Hallows had come straight from home and was waiting near No. 72 for me and Jewle's car. The car drew in at the kerb almost at once. I told Jewle it was uncommonly kind of him to go out of his way to do us a favour.

"As a matter of fact I'm a lot more implicated than when I saw you last," he said. "Can't tell you about it now, but it rather looks as if Wayner, the man who was caught here, is a long way off being an amateur. There may be a prior and more serious charge. That's confidential, of course."

Jewle said the Morren staff hours were usually from nine to six but he'd arranged for them to be early. Morren himself was rarely in before half-past nine or ten. At any rate it was Morren himself who admitted us that morning. He looked mightily surprised to see me. Jewle noticed it. He doesn't miss much.

"Mr. Morren and I have met before," I said. "Just the matter of vetting a small claim on United Assurance."

I introduced Hallows: said we were both there on behalf of the insurers. Handshakes, and we went through the outer door. Morren seemed almost a different man to me. He'd smiled courteously. He'd even said, and as if he really meant it, that he was very glad to see us.

The first thing we wanted was a knowledge of the lay-out. Face the two-storeyed building from across the street and the door was on the far left. When we went through, it was to a tiny lobby, with a notice which said "Please ring". In other words, a caller had to be admitted from the far side of the lobby door.

We went through to a larger lobby. To the left were the stairs. The short flight led to a landing from which a passage went right, to the door of the far room. To the right of the downstairs lobby was the cloakroom with lavatory and basin, and beyond it the cloakroom proper and a tiny kitchen with a gas-cooker. If one went across the lobby and kept left, one was in the main workroom.

We went up the stairs. The door at the head led to Morren's office. It had the usual furnishings plus a small bookcase of what seemed to be largely technical books.

"You see we've had the door repaired," Morren remarked to Jewle. "We got a man in after you left. And this door too."

He referred to a door that led from his office to that of his head man, a specialist in design named Ward. We went through to Ward's room. To the left was the window that overlooked the yard: the window through which Wayner had tried to make his escape. To the right was a door that opened on the passage that led back to the stairs. Ward, in other words, didn't have to go through Morren's room to get downstairs. He used that door.

Through the window we had a look at the concreted yard. Beyond it one could see the back gardens and back premises of the houses of Holloway Terrace. The eight-foot brick wall ran the whole way along what one might call Corby Street, but only one or two of the Corby Street premises seemed to have their yards entirely enclosed, like that of No. 72.

"It was my father who had the enclosure made about a couple of years before he died," Morren told us. "There used to be an outdoor lavatory there and a coal-shed before we had the whole place modernised. If you look just in front of the wall, Mr. Travers, you can see what looks like a stain. That's the blood from Wayner's hand when he tried to hoist himself up."

"You were rung about Wayner earlier this morning," Jewle said. "The name still conveys nothing to you?"

"Never heard it in my life. And nobody of his description ever called here. Ward confirms it and he's been my deputy ever since I took over."

Jewle asked if the three of us could use Morren's office for a minute or two. Morren left us to it. He'd shown Jewle the desk push-bell in case he himself should be wanted.

"Right," Jewle told me. "Doesn't matter about the rest of the premises. What you've seen is all that's needed to get a clear picture. So suppose you go into Corby Street and come up to the front door. You just walk in, but as soon as you step on the lobby mat a bell you can't hear rings in the downstairs workroom, so whoever's working there knows there's a caller. At the same time the caller himself confirms by ringing the wall bell as instructed. I think you'll agree that in a place like this that's an admirable precaution."

He gave his wry smile.

"Except for one thing. The front door has a Yale lock and the key was left in the lock on the inside. You can call it laziness or negligence, but that's how it was. Ward always arrived first, and it was his key that was left in the lock. He left last and took the key with him. Morren also had a key in case of any emergency. But you see the point?"

We did. All Wayner had had to do was open the front door some time and take an impression of the key.

"So far, so easy," Jewle went on. "That night he let himself in. Whether or not the mat bell rang didn't matter a damn. It was a misty night, and whether or not he was alone we can't say. In three seconds he could have been at the door, through it and with the door closed again. Unluckily for him, he didn't lock it, because he knew he might have to make a quick getaway.

"Right, then. He comes up the stairs and into here. He slips the bolts of the door and gets to work. When I say *he*, by the way, it might be *they*. Here's the safe."

The bookcase I've mentioned had four shelves and was about four feet high. You couldn't see that it had tiny runners till Jewle took hold of one side and swivelled the whole thing back from its recess. The safe itself was set partially in the wall behind it. There was nothing conspicuous about it. To me it was just a safe.

"He or they get to work," Jewle went on. "By this time our men are inside downstairs. There's a faint noise, so one begins mounting the stairs. He's heard from inside. Let's assume from now on there's two men at that safe. As soon as the door's rattled and the cop calls to his mate the two slip through here to where we are now—Ward's room. The bolts are pushed home and there's a second or two of deliberation. A look at that passage door, then, 'You try and make it downstairs and I'll try the window.' Morren's door has been crashed open and the cops are about to break in here. There's no one downstairs and the confederate makes his getaway with the diamonds. Wayner ups with the window and drops."

As I said, the whole thing was absolutely clear.

"Don't think I'm being obstinate," Hallows said, "but to me it doesn't make sense. Wayner's movements—yes. After all, he'd see what was through the window—except perhaps the broken glass on the wall—and his instinct would be to get out to the open air and a getaway in the dark. It's the confederate that's all wrong."

Jewle smiled. "I've a rough idea what you're going to say, but say it."

Hallows smiled too. "I will. And it's this. There's no doubt that when he or they got to the safe the diamonds were there?"

"None whatever. We've been on to Lorenz Brander in Birmingham and he confirms it. By the way, he'll be at the Yard later this morning."

"Right," Hallows said. "When the police broke in, the safe was already open?"

"It was."

Hallows shook an incredulous head.

"In a matter of seconds! The best man in the business couldn't have done it; filed fingertips, stethoscope and all. In those few seconds this safe couldn't have been opened. And yet it was. And I see only two ways. One is that it was deliberately left open by someone or other, and the other that the combination was known. You agree?"

Jewle shook his head. "It certainly wasn't left open. Morren closed it and no one else knew the combination—not even Ward."

He held up a hand. "Just a minute. Let me explain. The combination was changed every month, usually on the first, and so it was changed only a few days ago. Ward is told the combination only when Morren's away, and he hasn't been away at all since it was changed. Morren was the only one who could open this safe, and you can take my word for it that he closed it and had no possible means of opening it till after the robbery."

I asked if I might say something. What *was* the combination?

"An apt one for the new year—1962," Jewle said. "No use trying it. It's naturally been changed again."

Hallows was getting a bit restless. "Mind if we get back to what I was saying? Morren didn't open the safe, the cracksman hadn't time, so the only possible answer is that the combination was known. Isn't that so?"

"Well—yes."

"Very well then, so tell me this. If the combination was known, why did Wayner trouble to bring along someone to open the safe?"

For me that was a bit of a facer. Jewle gave his usual wry smile. "There's no honour among thieves. Two were there because each didn't trust the other."

"Sounds simple," I said, "when you say it like that."

I looked at my watch. It was just after ten o'clock. "Anything else here we ought to try to pick up for ourselves?"

"Don't imagine so," Jewle said. "I think I can supply you with everything."

Hallows asked about the employees. Jewle took out his notebook.

"George Ward's forty-two and he's been with the firm since he was nineteen. Percy Grover—who's a kind of head craftsman—is thirty-four and came here straight from Arts and Crafts School. Desmond Lever's nineteen, from the same school as Grover, who's his uncle. All are happy in their jobs. In our judgment they're none of them the kind to do anything crooked. To be more mundane, none knew the safe combination. Also all three left here together at about five minutes to six that night. They took a bus from the stop just down the road as they always did: went to King's Cross and from there Ward went on to Palmers Green and the other two to Golders Green. By that time the job here had been done."

"We'll take your word about the employees," I said. "But I've got an idea. When are you expecting Brander?"

"About half-past eleven."

"Then could we go somewhere and have a talk over coffee?"

He said he didn't know why not. There was nothing to keep him there.

As we went down the stairs Morren came through from the workroom. He was looking a bit worried as he asked if we'd any new ideas. I assured him that his claim ought to go through in a very few days.

"What'll you do for stones in the meanwhile?" Hallows asked him.

"No special difficulty at the moment. Those stones were really stock. But for what happened they'd have been in the bank as soon as it opened the next morning. Meanwhile, there're the usual channels. Also I've a rather important valuation later in the week and I've an idea the clients might want to dispose of certain objects. They often do."

"Well, we'll be going," Jewle said. "I expect you're pretty busy. Got much in hand?"

"Quite a lot," he said. "A pair of presentation caskets in silver, enamel and crystal. You'd like to see them as far as we've got?"

Good of him, Jewle said, but we were rather busy. Handshakes all round and we left.

We took Jewle's car. Not far from King's Cross the driver drew in at a teashop. Jewle sent him on to the Yard. We got a table to ourselves, and as soon as the coffee came I suggested to Hallows that I should tell Jewle about that job the previous November at Cockfosters. I went into it pretty fully but he didn't seem very impressed.

"What's the connection? I mean, you can't compare the two. Assume Mrs. Morren did help herself to a pretty big wad of household money, you can't be suggesting she was mixed up in this other affair?" He smiled. "How on earth *could* she have been involved?"

"Don't know," I told him frankly. "But two queer things have happened to the Morrens inside a couple of months. And don't forget something. She assured Vigors and me— to her husband's face, mind you—that he was forgetful and careless, so he might have left some memo lying around. Something giving the new combination of the safe."

"I see. And she passed it on. To whom? Wayner?" He smiled. "Or are you suggesting she was the confederate?"

"Now you're pulling my leg," I said. "All the same, there are two little things we haven't mentioned. She was the only one of the family who didn't go to the dinner with

Brander that night. I'd like to know what the previous engagement was that kept her away."

"We ought to learn that from Brander himself," he said. "Personally, though, I think you're barking up the wrong tree."

"There *is* one other little thing," Hallows said. "Who was the woman who tipped off the police?"

I won't say it pulled up Jewle with a jerk, but for the first time he looked as if he might take us seriously.

"That's something I'd very much like to know."

"Didn't you mention a Cockney accent?"

"My information was this," he said. "I can check on it later, but I think this is about right. The caller said. 'You the police, gov'ner? You'd better get a move on if you want to stop a job. At a place called Morren's. That's in Corby Street, Clerkenwell. Soon after six o'clock.' Then the caller rang off as soon as she was asked the usual question. After that the message was automatically passed on. You know the procedure. The accent was noted as slightly Cockney, but that didn't mean it wasn't phoney."

He looked at his watch.

"I take it you people would like to see Brander? If so, we'd better be getting along."

Jewle's sergeant was waiting for him with some papers. He said that Brander hadn't yet arrived. Jewle told him to get all he could on that 999 call.

"Excuse me," he told us. "These look as if they might be important."

He was still at it five minutes later when Brander was announced. He was an older man than Morren: burly, double-chinned, and his closely cropped hair a badger grey. He'd spent his young manhood in London and spoke English with only an occasional false intonation. His manner was genial. I liked him. When his immense hand gripped mine I was ready to wince, but it was no more than a handshake after all.

Jewle is big too, but he wasn't in the Brander class. He's the quiet type. He fits the cliché of well-disguised iron hand in velvet glove. No need, he told Brander, to inspect any credentials. The three of us were only too grateful for his help.

He passed the cigarettes. Brander took one. Hallows and I lighted up too, to show how cosy it all was.

"Just a brief statement," Jewle said largely, "and that's all." He turned to Hallows and me. "Mightn't it be better to put a few simple questions to Mynheer Brander so that he can make them the basis of a statement?"

We thought it a good idea.

"Then I'll make rough notes he can use later. That all right with you, Mynheer Brander?"

Brander thought the idea excellent.

"Then we'll begin with your visit to England. You don't come very often?"

He rarely came more than once a year. He said it was a sort of sentimental journey combined with a little business. He saw old friends, some in the trade and some not. In the case of his cousin Karl, it was very much a family visit, combined this time with the minimum of business. Karl knew when he'd be coming, and this time he'd mentioned an important commission for which he'd need stones. He'd written him that he'd definitely bring a selection.

He told us some people might regard him as a wealthy man, but, whether that were so or not, he was not prepared to make money out of his only surviving relative.

"To put it bluntly, your cousin got the stones more cheaply than if he'd bought them in the open market."

Brander said that was so. He'd brought a selection of stones and they'd spent a good hour over them in Karl's office. A selection had been made, Karl had given him a cheque and then the stones had been put in the safe.

"You actually saw it?"

"I did," he said. "And then the safe was properly closed and the bookcase put in place."

"Anyone else come into the office while you were there?"

"Oh yes," he said. "When we were half-way through, Mr. Ward brought some tea. He's a very old friend. I always make a point of seeing him. That's why he brought up the tea himself."

"And after the business was over?"

"Karl and I went downstairs and into the workroom. I saw the designs and had a word with Mr. Grover. He's also an old friend. The younger man I hadn't met before. I forget his name."

"Lever."

He smiled.

"Yes. Mr. Lever. A very nice young man. I think he's Mr. Grover's nephew."

"You're right," Jewle said. "And after that?"

After that he and Karl had a wash and brush-up, and then left for the hotel. It was a turn-and-turn about sort of arrangement which had somehow become the custom ever since Karl's children were of an age to appreciate it. One year he would spend the evening with Karl at his house and sleep there: the next year everyone would come to the hotel. He always used the same hotel.

"How do the children regard you?"

Brander laughed.

"They call me Uncle Lorenz. I think they're very fond of me." His expression sobered. "I'm very fond of them too. I'm a bachelor and to me they represent something more than Karl's children."

"Of course. And was it a surprise that Karl's wife wasn't able to be with you?"

"Not exactly," he said. "How can a visit of mine be expected to suit everybody's arrangements?"

"And you don't know why she couldn't come?"

"I didn't. Karl brought her love and said it couldn't be avoided. It was what you call 'one of those things'."

"And how were the children?"

He smiled. "They're still lovely children. I'll tell you something. Karl wished to call the boy Brander, after me, but his wife found it—well, not an English name, so we compromised. Bernard is an anagram of Brander. You didn't think of that?"

Jewle shook a rueful head. "A bit too clever for me. I take it you're very fond of him?"

"He's a fine boy. And doing very well."

Another smile.

"And Greta too. She was always a tomboy. I think she still is, even when she tries to be serious. They're fine children."

"I'm sure they are. And they must have been very excited when they knew you were coming over. They would know, of course?"

"Of course. Of course. It was a kind of event. Something like Christmas."

"With presents?"

He laughed. "Perhaps. But one shouldn't ask questions of your English Santa Claus."

That was about all. Jewle had a draft of the points Brander should mention in his statement. Brander looked at it and agreed.

"You gentlemen mind if I ask you a question? You think you will be able to recover those diamonds?"

"We're doing our best," Jewle said. "We realise that you yourself must feel very keenly about it. It won't be a loss, of course. The insurance will cover that. All the same, it's a most unpleasant business. And now, if you'll go with my sergeant, we'll say goodbye when I've seen your statement."

The two went out.

"A very nice man," Jewle told us.

We agreed. And, which was more important, most unlikely to let himself be involved in anything with even a suspicion of shadiness.

"You saw the point of all those questions? Only one thing now to clear up. You can call it a concession to you two, if you like, but I'm going to find out just what Mrs. Morren's prior engagement was."

I was already making for my hat and overcoat.

"Wait a minute," he said. "It'll be at least a quarter of an hour before Brander's statement is ready, so why not draw up a couple of chairs. I think I'm going to surprise you."

4. DAVID WAYNER

IT WAS an afternoon of late August and harvest around Insbury was in full swing. It's one of those communities that can't be called towns but seem too large for villages. Shops, of course: a hotel, a garage and two pubs. But no bank. Once a week a Watford bank opened its small rented premises for the convenience of its Insbury customers—on a Thursday from two o'clock till half-past three.

Insbury has one main or through street; a shopping area interspersed with private houses. Three or four side roads lead off and these are all residential. The fifteenth-century church lies at the west end, and just beyond it, in still open parkland, is a girls' school. It used to be Insbury Hall.

The room used by the bank had no back entrance. It was a room belonging to a small general store that occupied a corner of High Street and Hatchley Road. The room itself was fourteen feet by ten. You entered the door on High Street and in front of you, about eight feet away, was the counter. To the left was the only chair, generally occupied by a middle-aged man named Henry Burton. I suppose one could call him the guard. He also drove the car from Watford, helped the cashier to take in money, and then locked the car and left it parked in front of the door. The cashier that particular Thursday was a Roger Greenham. He was of medium height and spare. His age was twenty-five and he'd been with the bank for nine years.

The rest of the layout of the room was very simple. There was just a counter with a flap at the left through which the cashier used to take in money and hand out whatever it is a customer needs, and a second counter where money, various forms, new cheque-books and the usual pair of scales were kept. That Thursday most of the customers had done their business before three. Insbury lies in a farming community and most were too busy to do more than drive in and out. At three-twenty-five the cashier was already thinking of getting ready for the eight-mile journey home.

Then things happened, and quickly. A man entered. Burton was still reading a newspaper and Greenham was sorting some notes. The man was tallish. An old soft hat was well down over his eyes and a reddish handkerchief across the lower half of his face. He whipped down the blind to cover the glass of the door, turned the key and stood there, back to the door. It was all done so quickly that when Burton looked up to see what was happening to the door the man had a gun in his hand.

"This a hold-up. Don't move, you!" That was to Burton. "And you. Put those notes on the counter."

Burton made a mistake. He moved. As he rose he was caught by a left uppercut clean on the point of the jaw. It was a couple of minutes before he was able to move.

Greenham tried to take his time. The gunman warned him, but he still tried to save the day by putting the notes on his right of the counter and rather nearer his own side. As the gunman reached for them, Greenham grabbed the free arm. The gunman dropped the gun and, with the now free hands, seized him by the coat collar and almost dragged him across the counter. Greenham said afterwards he'd never thought it possible for a man to move so fast. By the soreness of his chin afterwards, he knew he, too, must have taken an uppercut clean on the point.

Burton came to first. The alarm was raised, but it was far too late. Notes to the value of almost eleven hundred pounds had gone. The gun, a wooden dummy, lay on the floor. But there had been two witnesses to the man's exit. A, a woman, had wondered why a man should be running from the bank and round to Hatchley Road. B, a driver employed by the store, was just in time to see the man literally jump into what looked like a small sports car. It was moving off as the man jumped in. B thought it a bit queer but forgot all about taking the car number. After all, he was busy loading his own little van with customers' orders.

A general correlation of evidence put the man as of slim build and almost six foot. His voice had been an assumed one—a kind of growl. He might have been about thirty years old, but was almost certainly, or had been, a professional boxer. That, at any rate, was all the police had to go on. There was no record of the numbers of the missing notes, which in any case were almost all old.

That was what Jewle told us and what we gathered later from the files of the local newspaper. With so little to go on, it was no wonder that the police got nowhere. It was a robbery carefully planned, executed with a minimum of fuss and leaving almost no clues.

So there we were in Jewle's room, listening to that story of the robbery of a small branch bank.

"Nothing. Just nothing," Jewle said. "Till last night about an hour after we broadcast that description of Wayner. Then who should ring but that cashier—Greenham. He said he'd given the local police a further clue. When the man reached for the notes right across the counter, the sleeve of his jacket was slightly drawn back, and when he grabbed the arm it went back further, and he definitely saw some tattooing just above the wrist. Everything else that was broadcast also seemed to fit Wayner.

"That was the trouble," Jewle went on. "The local police thought it all so vague as to be of virtually no importance. In any case, a so-called tattoo mark might be anything. Even if it had been identified as, say, a mermaid or an anchor or anything you like to mention, it couldn't have been all that help. But now, when you take into account everything else, the man has to be Wayner.

"And there *is* something else. You'd never guess it, but his father was a Colonel Wayner who used to live at Insbury Hall. Young Wayner must have been conversant with the operations of that little branch bank, and he certainly knew all the little local side roads and lanes when he made his getaway. All he'd have had to do before the robbery was make a quick check-up."

"Looks cut and dried," I said. "By the way, has he done any talking?"

"None," Jewle said. "What we hope is that his defence counsel will tell him what we now know and get him to ask for the robbery—and anything else he may have done—to be taken into account. There's plenty of time. As you've probably read, he's been remanded in custody till tomorrow week."

"Know any other facts about him?" That was Hallows.

Jewle smiled. "We do. Even arising out of what I've just told you, there's one very interesting fact. Think back, Bob. What was interesting about that hold-up?"

Hallows smiled a bit sheepishly.

"Can't say, except that it pinned another job on Wayner."

"Nothing else?"

Hallows laughed. It wasn't very heartily. "You're the one who's holding the cards. I can't see your hand—not all of it."

"But you did see it," Jewle told him. "Wayner left his car just round the corner and almost certainly with the engine slightly ticking over. It was on the move when he jumped in. And therefore?"

"Yes," Hallows said. "I see what you're driving at. He had a confederate."

"Exactly," Jewle said, and there wasn't the least note of triumph. "Do you think it might have been the same confederate who got away with the diamonds from Corby Street?"

There was a buzz. Jewle reached for the receiver. When he rang off he got to his feet.

"That was the Commander. Sorry I have to kick you out."

He didn't—not for the moment. There was a tap at the door and his sergeant came in with Brander and the statement. There were the usual formalities and then the goodbyes.

"This is what you should do," Jewle told us when everything was clear again. "Go and see a Harry Alders at The Carlo, Finsbury Park. Mention my name and he'll fill you in. Also the papers will have done some digging. They might have something by this afternoon."

We thanked him and left. In cases like the Corby Street break-in we're always at a disadvantage. People talk to the police, and if they don't there's always a little polite pressure. There's no such pressure that we can apply. People are willing to talk or else they hate to become involved. That's why our information is mostly second-hand. And why it's invaluable to have someone like Jewle. He knows it's a matter of mutual help. No one's trying to steal a march. So if Jewle was advising us to call on Harry Alders, then on Harry we'd be only too glad to call.

Hallows thought we ought to have lunch first. Harry's restaurant might be as good a place as any. Then he had another idea and rang The Carlo from Charing Cross Station. He looked pretty pleased when he came out of the phone box. Harry had asked us to have a meal on the house.

There was a time in my own Cambridge days when I was pretty keen on the boxing game, and it didn't take long for me to learn that that particular sport was about the worst I could have chosen. Six-foot-three and eleven stone cancelled each other out. There was the devil of a lot of me to hit for which length of reach didn't qualify, and I hadn't the weight or the speed for a compensatory counter-punch. Finally, a sparring partner caught me with a hefty right to the side of the head and when I got to my feet my eyes seemed a bit groggy. That's why, without my horn-rims, I'm now almost as blind as a bat. And why boxing ceased to interest me, especially when I took up golf instead. Golf-balls don't retaliate. They can't hit back.

We walked through to Leicester Square and took the Tube to Finsbury Park, and Bob Hallows told me all he knew about Harry Alders. Harry was an East Ender and got his first chance at the old Blackfriars Ring. George

Prentiss, the well-known light-heavy, took an interest in him, and when he left the game he became Harry's manager. Within a couple of years Harry held the British and European titles, and he retained them till a leg injury in a car accident put him out of the game. But he'd made a lot of money and, as Hallows had said, he'd been careful. Hence, among other things, The Carlo.

"His wife's family name," Hallows told me. "She was Soho-Italian. I met her only once and she struck me as the quiet, sensible type. Harry couldn't have picked a better. Unfortunately they had no children. That's why Harry does quite a lot for East End kids."

At the exit from the station we turned left, and it was only a minute's walk to Harry's place. It looked to me as if that old skating rink hadn't so much been renovated as reconstructed. From the outside it looked like a huge, ultra-modern cinema with swing entrance doors and an enormous foyer. To the left were the stairs down to the restaurant. To the far right was Harry's office. That was where an attendant took us. Harry was waiting for us.

I hadn't known the kind of man to expect, but to me he was a genuinely pleasant surprise and I'd taken strangely to him almost as soon as we'd shaken hands.

"A nice place you've got here, Harry," Hallows told him, looking round that office.

"It's handy," he said. "Not altogether my line, but you have to keep up some sort of a front. What'll you two gents drink?"

We each settled for a dry sherry. Harry himself had more splash than whisky. I'd had a good look at him while he was getting the drinks. It was obvious he couldn't have made his old-time weight. He turned out to be the kind who rarely laughs, and he just smiled and shook his head when Hallows called him portly and prosperous. Certainly I'd never have taken him for an old-time pro. What he was, and as if he neither knew it nor cared, was just Harry Alders. There were, for instance, traces of Cockney he made no attempt to disguise. He was genuine. That's what I was to like about him.

I thought it best to get everything on a right footing. He knew, of course, why we'd wanted to see him.

"Bob told me," he said. "It's that diamond robbery. You're investigating for the insurance company. Mind if we leave it till a bit later?"

It was almost a gentle reproof. Hallows cut in with an inquiry after George Prentiss. Harry said he was well, but for trouble with his eyes. He and his wife were looking after a holiday camp for children down at Bognor. From what Hallows had told me, I had a shrewd idea who was financing it.

"He was a great lad, George," Hallows said. "One of the best. They don't make 'em like him, not any more."

They began talking about the fight game. Five minutes of that and Harry looked up at the clock.

The restaurant was very large, with the near end a dance floor and the smaller half the restaurant proper. It might have been any good-class West End place: lighting, decor, service—everything. Harry said it had been planned with the West End trade in mind. Handiness to the Tube station made it accessible. Prices for dinner-dances had been kept well below those of town and, in spite of the fact that he always used a reputable band, so far it had paid off. The patrons were mostly the younger, middle-class type, with no beatniks allowed and the long-haired types carefully scrutinised. Soon after the opening there'd been occasional trouble but none since.

I won't say it was the best lunch I've ever eaten but it was quite good. The wine list looked formidable but we drank ice-cold lagers. It was when the hors-d'oeuvres plates had gone and we were waiting for the next course that Harry suddenly mentioned David Wayner.

"I take it you'd like me to tell you about Dave."

I said, and it must have been apologetically, that it was up to him, but we'd be grateful. From then on he talked with only a rare interruption. He spoke slowly and carefully, as if he'd known what we'd really come for and was trying to keep to the script he'd had not too much time to prepare.

"I'd been asked down to Cambridge. I was a big name then and they asked me to M.C. a charity show. There was a welter there I liked. That was Dave Wayner. He looked to me like a first-class prospect for the Amateurs, so I had a word with him after the show. I had a place then at Royston, not so far away, so I suggested he should look me up there. Even then he was a likeable young chap. No side at all.

"As a matter of fact, he came to see me a few weeks later. In the January it was. I was training pretty hard for a fight with Tommy Dane—you may remember him, Bob—and he took a room for a week at the local hotel. I kidded him into sparring with me occasionally for a change, and he was good. Reflexes like lightning and an overhead cross you had to watch. Of course he wasn't in condition, but it was there and I told him so, but he wouldn't take it seriously. Too much money, I guessed.

His mother was dead but his father had plenty. And too many other interests. Even then he liked a fast car.

"The next I heard, only a week or two after the fight, was that his father had died. Mind you, what I'm telling you now was what I learned later, but the trustees were paying him an allowance till he was twenty-one, when he'd come into the money. He left Cambridge, if that's what you call it; and what with the allowance and what he raised from the sharks on his expectations, he was having a good time.

"I don't know what he actually did, but he never missed a fight of mine in town. He'd come down to the dressing-room afterwards and more than once he insisted on taking me and George out to dinner. It'd be at some posh West End place where everybody knew him. The wife got to know him too. She got quite fond of him, same as I did.

"Then I lost sight of him. That was after he came into that big wad of money. All we ever heard of him was when he sent us presents at Christmas. No address, but one postmark was Monte Carlo. Just 'Love from Dave'. That was up to two years ago. I'd been out of the game for quite a time then and I'd opened this place. I remember there hadn't been any presents the previous Christmas, but, all the same, you could have knocked me down with a feather when one afternoon he walked into this office. Remember that laugh, clown, laugh business? That's what he made me think of. He looked a bit seedy, but I couldn't believe it when he told me he was stone broke. He'd heard about my gymnasium and he asked me to give him a job. I tell you, I could have cried."

It was a moment or two before he went on.

"So I found him a job upstairs. Sandy Scott's my manager—you remember him, Bob—and Dave was sort of handyman under Sandy. Sandy liked him too. He got Dave back into shape. Later he began sparring with some of the customers Sandy was trying to bring along. Everyone liked Dave. Mind you, he was still the gentleman. No side, but you could tell he had class. Sometimes he'd come down here when he hadn't nothing else on and dance for an hour or two. To me he was just like a son. That's why I couldn't believe it when he told me he might be leaving."

"When was that?"

"Two days before this robbery. He said a relative in America wanted him to pay a visit, so he might be gone for some time. He mightn't even come back. I tell you I was worried. I had been for some time. Twenty quid a week, all found, was what I paid him, but the kind of clothes he bought, and other things, made me wonder where the money was coming from. I went into it confidentially with Sandy, but everything was in order here. I couldn't speak to Dave direct. It takes a bit of doing to ask anyone questions like that: all we could do was hope it was all on the level. And then this business turned up. It sort of left us numb. We just couldn't believe it. Dave couldn't have done a thing like that. Not Dave."

"I know," I told him quietly. "The trouble is that he did. He was caught red-handed."

"Yes," he said. "The Superintendent told me."

"You think we should tell Mr. Alders about that other affair?" I asked Hallows.

"Why not?" he said. "It's bound to come out."

So I told Harry about that bank hold-up. He listened very quietly.

"Eleven hundred pounds," he said. "Early in September he bought himself a nearly new Jaguar. Got it from the Park Garage just opposite the station. He was quite frank about it. Maybe he thought the proprietor—Fred Fellows—might have told me. I know Fred pretty well. At any rate, he said the trustees had dug up some more money and he'd spent it on the car."

"Know where the car is now?"

"I don't," he said. "I had a word with Fred only this morning and he told me Dave had sold it back at the end of October."

We went into that matter of the confederate. Harry couldn't help us. He knew nothing of Dave's friends or acquaintances—outside The Carlo. Until the police had rung him, he'd never heard the name Morren.

All that had brought us to the end of the meal. Coffee had come and I was just lighting my pipe when a waiter said I was wanted on the phone. I took the call at the cashier's desk. It was Jewle, only wanting to know if Alders was with us. Would I ask him to be in at around four o'clock when he—Jewle—wanted a word or two.

I remembered a question I ought to have asked Brander. He hadn't yet gone back to Amsterdam, Jewle said. He himself had been talking to him, and he wasn't taking a plane before morning.

"As a matter of fact he's having Morren's two children to tea at the Eversleigh this afternoon."

I thought it best that he should hear from Alders himself, and not from me, about that Jaguar Wayner had bought in September, so I rang off. There was also something slightly disturbing that was happening under my nose. The girl at the desk—a pretty brunette—had been looking at an evening paper when I'd come to the phone, and now she was furtively wiping her eyes. I mentioned it to Harry when I was back at the table.

"That's Maria, my wife's niece. Excuse me."

He went to the desk. His back was to us and partly concealed her. He might have been cajoling or reprimanding, but when she stood up he patted her shoulder and watched her as she went to the door and out. He still stood there, and then another girl, a tall blonde, appeared and Harry came back.

"I'd like you to keep it to yourself," he said, "but that was about Dave. She was reading about him and it upset her."

"You mean?"

He guessed what I meant.

"It was her fault. I told her so. Just because he took her out once or twice, that didn't make him serious. Maria's a nice girl, a good-looking girl, but I told her. He wasn't her sort. All he was doing was being friendly."

He was looking upset all the same.

"Forget it," I told him. "It's no business of ours. And now we ought to be going."

He protested. He wanted to show us the rest of the place, so we went upstairs. We took only a peep into the bowling alley. Only three or four lanes were being used, but by early evening, he said, there'd be queues. It was the first bowling alley I'd seen, except on television. He said it had its own snackbar for those who might find the restaurant too expensive.

We went upstairs to the gymnasium with its faint smell of sweat and embrocation. As far as I could see, it had everything. Things were busiest in the morning. Pretty busy in the evenings too, only a different kind of client. To our left was quite a large, partitioned-off space. Two rooms there, he said. Dave had had one and Sandy Scott, the gym manager, used the other as an office. The police had been over Dave's room, though what they'd expected to find he didn't know.

We said goodbye in the foyer.

"You've got a wonderful place here, Harry," Hallows told him. "I'm glad it's doing well."

Harry smiled. "Yes, it's a nice place. We try to keep it like that. You'd like one like it?"

"It's an idea. All I'd want is money."

"Do what I did," he said. "Find yourself a nice bank manager."

We laughed. I had a last, serious word. He could still assure me he had no idea who David Wayner's confederate might have been.

"No," he said. "Dave knew everybody here. And everybody knew Dave. What happened when he wasn't here, don't ask me. I wouldn't know."

I thanked him for the hospitality and he seemed a bit embarrassed. There was one last word. He asked us to let him know anything new about Dave that could safely be passed on.

We went out to the comparative drabness of the street.

"What a bloody fool that Dave Wayner must have been!"

That was Hallows, and somehow it was an epitome of the last two hours.

We called at the Park Garage and saw Fellows, the proprietor. He confirmed the transactions with the

Jaguar. He'd liked Dave Wayner and occasionally let him have a car on a free afternoon.

We asked him only two more questions. Had he any idea who the confederate might have been? Did Wayner, for instance, ever bring a friend along to the garage?

Fellows knew of none.

Then would he tell us the reasons Wayner gave—if he gave any—for parting with the Jaguar after only a couple of months?

"I think he was in bad with his bookie," he said. "I know from things he told me. Also I'd have given him more for the Jag than he asked."

It wasn't far off four o'clock when we got back to the agency. Hallows said he'd make a brief précis of the afternoon and phone it to Jewle later. There might be something for us in return. I said I was calling it a day.

I don't quite know why I was keeping it to myself, but I had something in mind. There were two people whom I'd never yet seen—the Morren children, and, since I had that important question to ask Brander, I thought I'd try to gatecrash that tea-party at the Eversleigh. If it didn't succeed, then a chance might present itself later, but with luck in the timing I thought I might pull it off.

So I went home and dolled myself up a bit. I rang the hotel and did some careful questioning. Then I collected my car and drove to the Eversleigh. It was then a quarter-past five and the rain was coming down in sheets.

5. OWL AMONG THE NIGHTINGALES

They rang from the desk and I was told to go up. Room 169 was on the third floor. It was really a small suite; of lounge, bedroom and bathroom. Brander himself opened the door. I don't know why, but he seemed quite pleased to see me.

"Come in, Mr. Travers. Let me take your hat and coat. We were just talking about you."

All traces of the tea had gone. Brander was smoking a cigar. Bernard Morren and his sister were smoking cigarettes.

"No, really not," I said. "I'm staying only just long enough to ask you a question. It was unpardonable butting in like this."

He took my hat and coat and literally made me sit down. That small lounge was comfortably furnished as hotel lounges go. I took the settee with Greta. She was a striking-looking girl: shortish, blonde hair swept back from the neck, large, soulful eyes and a complexion that had almost a bloom. The brother was of medium height and rather thick-set. He might have been any young City executive.

I said I'd already had tea but I accepted a cigarette from the case that Bernard offered.

"This is really most exciting," Greta said. "Uncle Lorenz was just telling us about you. You're working for the insurance company about poor Daddy's diamonds."

"You're trying to recover them, aren't you, sir?"

That was Bernard Morren. Both had the assured, cultured voices of the modern, well-to-do young: voices which in some queer way make a man of my age seem hopelessly out of things: voices that can sustain a cause without the aid of logic: that somehow put you at a disadvantage before you've even begun to state a case. They may not be in the least obtrusive but there's a kind of built-in omniscience.

"Nothing exciting about it," I said. "It's just asking questions and more questions. Sometimes you get answers: most times you don't."

Bernard asked me if I'd actually seen Wayner. I said I hadn't. He was being held pending the trial.

"A funny thing about him," Bernard said, "he was actually at my college. Before my time, of course, but he still had quite a reputation. I suppose you weren't at Cambridge, sir?"

"Don't be so superior," Greta told him. "Why shouldn't Mr. Travers have been at Cambridge?"

"I wasn't trying to be superior," he told her quietly. "It was merely a form of question."

"As a matter of fact, I was," I said, and that meant talking Cambridge for a minute or two. Greta was listening with a kind of cynical amusement.

"And you, Miss Morren? Are you at Cambridge?"

"Heavens, no!" she said. "I'm trying to be a couturière. I was at an art school."

"They teach that at art school?"

"But of course. Weaving, fabric printing, dress-making, millinery, cutting, designing—everything."

"Just shows how ignorant a man like me can be. And now you're working in a boutique, if that's what it's called?"

"It's actually Helen Cambon," she said. "That's the name, of course. Helen Cambon—her father was French—

and Grace Wilde are the actual partners. It's in Gordon Street. Do you know it?"

"I can find it. In any case I'll tell my wife about it."

You'd have thought I'd given her a blank cheque. She put her hands together as if in ecstasy.

"You're a darling. But be sure to tell her to say I sent her."

Bernard laughed. "Greta, you certainly don't miss a trick. Excuse her, Mr. Travers. She *will* try a bit too hard."

She made a face at him.

"But, seriously, we do turn out some marvellous stuff. We're having our own show in the autumn. Tremendously exciting."

I'd glanced at Brander. He'd been left out of things but he didn't seem to mind. He'd just sat there, smoking placidly and listening with an avuncular interest. He caught my eye.

"Greta's a clever girl," he told me. "It may not be long before she's a partner too."

"Not for years yet," she said. "Not unless Daddy finds a whole lot of money."

There was a knock. She was on her feet at once and making for the door.

"That's Frank!"

She was taller than I'd judged and she had a lovely figure. The man at the door looked rather older than Bernard. He had reddish hair, and the slightly snub nose gave his face a kind of amiability.

"Sorry I'm so late," he said. "It just couldn't be helped."

She stretched up and kissed his cheek.

"You poor dear. But come and meet Uncle Lorenz."

So that was the reason for the little party. Frank Sievers. Someone—Karl Morren?—had mentioned his interest in Greta. The family owned jewellers' shops in town, and he was wearing an Old Reptonians' tie. Greta might be doing pretty well for herself.

Bernard had just grinned and waved a hand at Sievers as he came in. It was Brander who introduced me. Bernard added his little piece.

"Mr. Travers is working for the insurance company, trying to recover those damn diamonds."

Sievers looked only politely surprised. There was ample room for three on the settee, and he sat down between me and Greta.

"Really? I can't say I envy you, Mr.—Sorry, I just didn't catch your name."

"Travers, darling," Greta told him. "Mr. Travers is a very charming man."

He looked the least bit sheepish.

"I'm sure he is. I mean—"

"Never mind, darling. He really dropped in to ask Uncle Lorenz something."

"Only a very simple question," I said. "Actually it might interest all of us. It was whether or not your uncle, here, could identify any of the missing diamonds."

Brander laid the cigar down. It was little more than a butt in any case.

"Three of them—yes. Up to tomorrow—yes. After that, perhaps not. Thousands of stones go through my hands. There'd have to be a very special reason to make me remember."

"But surely there was a special reason, Uncle," Bernard pointed out. "The diamonds were stolen."

"But that was afterwards. At the time it was just an ordinary transaction between your father and myself."

"But surely there're differences," Greta said, and gave a quick look at Sievers for confirmation. "There's the weight and how they're cut, and the colour."

"You're out of your depth," Bernard told her.

"I don't know," Sievers said. "What do you say. Mr. Brander?"

"In a way Greta's right," he said. "But why did you ask, Mr. Travers?"

"The police might recover some stones at some time or other and naturally they'd try to find out where they came from. Also these missing stones will be passed on by the fence and may be used. If the police recover stolen jewellery, an identification of the actual stones could lead to the apprehension of the original thief."

"But the police know who the thief was," Sievers said. "Maybe," I said. "But Wayner—the man they caught red-handed—definitely didn't have the stones on him. That's why the police are pretty sure he had an accomplice."

I got to my feet. "Now I really have to be going. In any case, it was unpardonable of me butting in as I did."

Greta sprang up. "But we're all going. Uncle Lorenz has a dinner engagement, haven't you, Uncle?"

"Is it still raining?" I asked Sievers.

"Was when I came in. Just pelting down."

"Then can I give you people a lift? Where're you actually going?"

"Just along Flagon Street," Bernard said. "To my place."

"But that's on my way," I said. "I can drop all three of you there."

The farewells had already begun. Greta kissed her uncle on the cheek and his arm went round her for a moment, and he was smiling. He said something. I didn't hear it. It might have been in Dutch. At any rate, she kissed him again.

"Don't forget to come to us next year," Bernard said as he shook hands. Then he smiled. "But for God's sake don't bring father any more diamonds!"

Sievers shook hands. "It was nice to see you, sir. Hope to see you again when you come next time."

Hats and coats had been deposited in the bedroom. I said goodbye to Brander myself. He gave a wry smile as he shook my hand.

"Ah, these children!" he said. "Always in a hurry."

"Give them time," I said. "Once we were in a hurry ourselves."

Greta gave a little sigh when we were making for the lift.

"Uncle's an old dear but he can be a bit of a bore," she told Bernard. "Do you think that's why Mummy hasn't any use for him?"

"Between you and me, I don't think he's ever been too enthusiastic about *her*," Bernard said. "You've got to admit it was damn bad manners not turning up the other night. She might have put off her damn bridge for once."

"If it *was* bridge, darling."

Incredible, in a way. I mightn't have been there. On the ground floor I suggested they should wait while I brought the car round from Dryden Street. The rain was still coming down in sheets as they got in: Greta and Sievers at the back and Bernard up front with me. He said he'd show me the way. It might be a bit tricky, what with the rain and the traffic.

It was he who lost his way. There wasn't much traffic till we managed at last to turn into Regent Street. It was the second on the left, he said, when we were in the main stream. Once in Flagon Street, things were easier. The two in the back seemed oblivious to where we were. Greta had her head on Sievers's shoulder. That much I could see in the mirror.

There was only an occasional car and I could relax. I could even take a look when Bernard drew my attention to a building on the right.

"That's where I work. London Publications."

The street narrowed as we neared Flagon Street. He told me to slow at the crossroads, then to keep in at the kerb. Fifty yards on and we were at No. 97. We'd hardly stopped when the couple behind were out of the car and making for the side door of a bookshop. Bernard was sitting tight.

"Look, sir, you really must come in for a drink. You've been so awfully decent and we'd appreciate it."

"That's very kind, but what're you young people doing?"

"Don't worry about us," he said. "We're going to a show, but not for another hour at least."

"Then perhaps for a few minutes. It's very kind of you."

He waited till I'd locked the car. The light was on in the passage and you could clearly see the stairs. It was quite light on the landing with the apartment door open.

Greta was probably in her room. Sievers had taken off his overcoat and was manipulating the electric fire.

Bernard took our hats and coats into what I guessed must be his bedroom.

"What a charming apartment!"

"It is rather nice," Sievers said. "Bernard was lucky to get it. The bookshop belongs to his firm, and then the two girls who were there moved to a place further along. Just in time."

The lounge—one stepped straight into it from the landing—was about fifteen by ten. Morren must have spent quite a bit on it. Besides comfortable things on which to sit, including a handsome pouffe, it had a radiogram, television set, telephone, and a showy piece of furniture that looked like a reproduction commode but turned out to be a cocktail cabinet.

"What'll you drink, sir?"

"Gin, if you have it. And French."

Sievers laughed. He had an attractive, almost boyish face. "You ask for it: he has it. I'll have vodka and a dash of rum."

Greta came in through the right of the two doors at the end of the room, almost certainly the spare bedroom. She asked Sievers what he was having and said she'd have the same. Bernard had a gin and tonic, and we got ourselves seated.

"Something I've been bursting to ask you, sir," Sievers said. "I don't know if it's in order, but mightn't this chap Wayner split on his accomplice, or whatever you call him, if he was to be promised a lighter sentence? I mean, mightn't that lead to the recovery of the diamonds?"

I told him it wasn't so easy as that. His counsel might tactfully suggest it, but hardly the police. The laws on the taking of evidence, and interrogation, were exceedingly strict. A case against a prisoner, for instance, could be wholly invalidated if you attempted to play off an accomplice against him, and vice versa.

"Just shows how much you don't know," Bernard said. "But what about you? You think you've got a chance of finding something out?"

"There's always that," I said. "It might take an awful long time, but there's always a chance. It might be tomorrow, or next year—"

"Sounds like a pop song," Greta said. "Or that tearjerker Vera Lynn used to sing: *Don't know where, don't know when.*"

She began to hum the tune.

"For God's sake be quiet," Bernard told her sharply. "Can't you be serious for once?"

"As a matter of fact, I thought it was rather apt," I said. "But, seriously, I suppose none of you people ever saw anything suspicious?"

"Wait a minute," Bernard said. "There was one thing. You tell him, Greta. You know. About Scruffy."

"Oh yes," she said. "That was really something out of a thriller. Even you saw that. But it was like this. I came home one evening—it was last March—and I was a bit early, really, and there was no one in the lounge and then I heard someone talking in the breakfast-room, so I listened. It was Mummy and some man or other. He had an awfully crude voice. She was thanking him, and then he said if ever she wanted anything again he'd be only too glad to oblige. That looked as if he was going, so I slipped out by the front door and waited till I could hear steps on the path from the breakfast-room, and I really got a good look at him as we passed. He had a Charlie

Chaplin moustache and an old-fashioned overcoat with a velvet collar and he was—well, scruffy. Mummy was in the lounge when I went in and I said, 'Who was that scruffy-looking man I met just now coming round from the back?' And she said, 'What on earth are you talking about?' Then she said it must have been someone who'd been seeing Albert. He's the gardener. But I ask you!"

"And you never found out who he was?"

She shrugged her shoulders. "How could I? I couldn't call Mummy a liar. I did have a word confidentially with Albert and he hadn't seen him. Also May, that's his wife, hadn't let him in. So he must have had instructions to go straight to the breakfast-room."

I smiled. "But surely your mother couldn't possibly be doing anything—well, underhand. There must be an explanation somewhere."

"You don't know Mummy," she said, and got to her feet. "Put on a record, Frank. You dance, Mr. Travers?"

"Too old and decrepit," I said.

"Let's go to my room," Bernard said. "We shan't be able to hear ourselves talk. And let me give you a refill."

He showed me through the other far door into his bedroom, and in a minute came in with my drink and another for himself. It was quite a small room with a single bed along one wall, and a minimum of furniture. Another door led through to the bathroom. The walls were almost covered with framed photographs, school and college groups mostly, but on the wall at the foot of the bed was a really charming water-colour of the Cockfosters house seen from the back gardens.

He told me to take the chair. He shifted the hats and coats and sat on the bed. The music from the lounge could easily be heard, but inside it must have been pretty strident.

"I don't know about you, sir," he said, "but I can't stand that damn stuff." He raised his glass. "Cheerio again."

"Tell me about yourself," I said. "How you're making out with your firm?"

"Nothing much to tell," he said. "Not yet. I'm beginning on the ground floor, so to speak, and working my way up. Getting what they call a general picture."

"You ever thought of doing any writing?"

He smiled a bit sheepishly. "To tell the truth, I have. I'm actually trying to work on something now. Only a sort of spy-cum-thriller."

"Why not," I said. "I hate intellectual arrogance. And there seems to be quite a lot of money in good-class spy stuff these days."

"You'd never guess how I got the idea. It was through Scruffy."

I must have stared.

"True," he said. "It was pretty queer if you come to look at it. I sort of tried to work it out and then one thing led to another and—well, that's how I began the book."

"Fine," I said. "If you were to use a pseudonym you could bring in this diamond business. Which reminds me of something. You're the kind of chap who could puzzle out how Wayner and his friend knew the combination of your father's safe."

"Yes," he said, and he was suddenly looking more serious. "Could I tell you something in strict confidence?"

"You definitely can."

"Then it's this," he said. "I've been doing some thinking about that. Thought it might be useful in a book, only

I can't very well use it. It's this. This last New Year's Day as ever was, Father and Greta and I were just about to have breakfast. I'd been home for the night and Mother never gets up much before ten. I remember I said something facetious, like, 'Well, here we are at jolly old 1962!' Father said, '1962', just as if he'd had an idea. Then he asked me how many permutations there'd be in those four numbers. I never was any good at maths, so I said I didn't know, but there'd certainly be dozens. And I asked why, and he said it'd be a handy set of numbers to use for the combination of his safe."

"Interesting," I said. "May I tell you something in even stricter secrecy?"

He nodded.

"1962 *was* the combination of the safe when it was opened that night."

"Good God!" He stared. "Father must have mentioned it to someone else. I'll tell you why. He used to change the combination of that safe at the beginning of every month. I think he used to do it sort of haphazardly. Any old numbers, and then that mention of 1962 gave him an idea to make things sort of routine. And easier. He *was* rather cock-a-hoop about it with Greta and me."

We agreed it still didn't explain how the combination could have got to Wayner and his partner. I thought I'd better leave things there.

"That's a lovely water-colour you have."

"It's our place at Cockfosters. It is rather nice. Done by one of Father's friends. You interested in colour photography? I've some rather nice ones of the house and so on. They're in this drawer. Haven't had time to mount them yet."

They were the usual smallish colour prints. The colours were good and they were remarkably clear: views of the gardens, some interiors, the married couple at the side door, little family groups, two or three of Karl Morren and a very good one of Beryl with Greta standing at her elbow. We were so engrossed that we didn't realise that the music had stopped. Greta looked in.

"Hurry up, Bernard. It's time to powder your nose."

I began apologising. Said how sorry I was to have stayed so long. He looked round for my hat and coat. I slipped that picture of Beryl Morren into my pocket. Then Frank Sievers came in.

"Look," I said, "can't I drop you people at wherever it is you're going?"

"No, no, no!" Bernard said. "Greta might be the devil of a long time yet. We'll ring for a taxi. If the rain's stopped we might even walk."

A kind of conspiratorial glance was exchanged as Bernard and I shook hands. He said I really must lunch with him some time. I said he and Sievers must have a meal at my club. Greta must have been in her room.

The rain was less heavy. I drove on to New Bond Street and to the garage where I parked the car. When I got to the flat, Bernice was all worried about me. I was almost two hours late and she'd expected me to telephone. I told her about Helen Cambon. Any excuse, however expensive, is better than none.

Most of my thinking is done when I feel the warmth of my bed. Unless the problem is a tricky one, it's an excellent recipe for sleep, and night after night I drop off in almost a matter of seconds. That night it took me a bit longer.

I began by trying to make an assessment of what I'd learned. One definite thing was that the sympathies of those two children—in the obviously strained relationships between their parents—lay with their father. And it explained why Greta spent so many nights in Bernard's apartment.

When I looked back I could still find something most interesting, even fascinating, about those Morren children, if only because it was quite a time since I'd come into such close contact with their generation. They were undoubtedly clever, with Greta the more direct. Bernard was the more likeable and she the more immediately attractive. Sievers would be at least ten years older: good-mannered and generally agreeable in a negative sort of way.

I began thinking about Scruffy and trying to imagine him. Greta's story had rung true: if it hadn't, I'd never have pocketed that photograph. Then, while I was trying to visualise the Cockfosters house and the path round to the breakfast-room. I fell asleep.

6. THE THEORY

Norris rang me just after breakfast the next morning in case I should want to change any plans. Hallows had been called away the previous evening on an enquiry into a somewhat suspicious fire. He's our arson expert and an enquiry like that might take quite a time, which meant that I'd have to carry on alone with the Morren diamonds case. Not that there seemed a great deal for me to do. The case had reached that exasperating point when you do things more as routine or for the sake of doing them than with any great hope that something must emerge. Overnight I'd had the glimmerings of a theory. Now, in the cold light of that January morning, it looked less like a theory than a jumble of ideas.

Norris did add something else—that United Assurance were offering a reward of £500 for information that might lead to the recovery of the diamonds. Even that had the look of a formality. If what had been stolen had been, say, a small collection of jewellery, a reward might have been something of a temptation. It might, for instance, have avoided the use of a fence. But loose diamonds were very different. No need whatever to worry about a market.

And there was something else to cast a bit of a damper. The robbery hadn't been one of those complex affairs involving a number of men, split-second organisation and complex material: the robbery, for instance, of a bank or a high-class jeweller's where thousands of pounds were involved. In other words, there wasn't a weak, human link: a someone who, for the sake of £500, might split on his pals or drop a quiet hint.

The Morren job was nothing like that. It was already not important enough to command even a mention in the papers, and that was how I had to look at it myself. Putting it very simply, it amounted to just this: that, through some contact unknown to us, Wayner had heard of the Morren premises as a likely prospect for a quick haul. All he would have to know, in order to start him thinking, was that the supposedly import firm were really manufacturing jewellers. Also those premises were not in, say, the busiest part of the city or the West End, but in a comparatively quiet, almost suburban road. So the two—Wayner and a confederate—had got to work on plans. What they'd expected as a haul was probably a certain amount of precious metals and some stones. There was no proof that on the night when the job was actually done they'd expected to find £10,000 worth of diamonds. That had been a stroke of luck.

That was what you might call a rough idea or a superficial view of things, but when you began to probe a bit everything wasn't so patent. Take one point only, which was the flaw on which my beginnings of a theory had been based. How had the combination of the safe been acquired?

I repeat—discounting the theory that the confederate had entered first and had had the safe open at the very moment of Wayner's entry—how had Wayner known what the combination was? And, in close conjunction, who was the third party who had known about the whole business and had seen that Wayner was shopped?

As for the combination of the safe, Jewle had been most emphatic when vouching for the absolute integrity of Morren's staff. So that left just four people—the Morren family. Take away those who couldn't possibly have been involved—Morren himself and the two children—and only Beryl Morren was left. And she was the only one who hadn't been that night at the Eversleigh Hotel. From what I'd heard Bernard say to his sister, an engagement at bridge had been the excuse. And that—though not so clearly as I've just stated it—was what had been at the back of my mind when I'd pocketed that photograph of Beryl Morren and her daughter in her son's bedroom. That, and yet another new and surprising factor: the entrance on the scene of the man whom Greta had called Scruffy.

What had a man like that been doing for Beryl Morren, and why had she lied to her daughter about him? Those were two questions to which I'd have liked the answers. Not that I didn't have answers of a kind. The trouble was that they weren't too convincing.

For example, assume that Beryl Morren had helped herself to that missing £200 from the safe at The Elms, then it must have been some financial difficulty that had made her do it. But she might have been in similar trouble much earlier, in the March of that same year when Greta had accidentally discovered a connection with Scruffy. Suppose that that March Beryl had decided to dispose of some of her jewellery and that she had answered one of those advertisements that frequently appear in the newspapers, and that the representative who had turned up at The Elms that March afternoon had been Scruffy. After their business had been concluded he had told her he'd be happy to be of service at any future time.

Suppositions are the raw material of theory, so let's go on supposing—that, for instance, Beryl Morren spotted in Scruffy a dishonest streak or, shall we say, no aversion to making a dishonest penny, and that a chance presented itself for using him later on. That was when she was in financial difficulties again.

What she did with what must have been ample spare time I had no idea. Bridge wouldn't have occupied the whole of it. Maybe she occasionally visited a gaming club, alone or with friends. Maybe she and some of those friends had patronised The Carlo. There she might have met Wayner. A friendship had begun. They'd understood each other, and when Beryl knew that for the month of January the combination of the Corby Street safe would be 1962, and that Lorenz Brander was about to pay his annual visit, then she took Wayner into her confidence and the whole thing was fixed up.

And so to the double-cross. There was someone else in whom Beryl confided, and that was Scruffy. It was he who entered the premises the moment the staff had left, and he who took the diamonds. Meanwhile Beryl tipped off the police, and when Wayner arrived it was to find an empty safe. Beryl and Scruffy had shared, or would share, what the diamonds fetched and Wayner would be nicely out of the way for quite a few years.

And why hadn't Wayner blown the gaff? Maybe he didn't know that he'd been shopped. And he was persistently keeping his mouth shut because—as Beryl had guessed—he was still too much of a gentleman to betray a lady. Either that or he hadn't the faintest notion what it was on that night that had gone so incredibly wrong.

So much, then, for the theory. The very first thing I did that morning was to take that picture of Beryl Morren and Greta to the firm of photographers we occasionally employ. I wanted half a dozen prints of Beryl alone, not necessarily in colour, and I was promised them for the midday.

At the agency I rang Jewle. He told me he had now no personal interest in the case but could, if necessary, bring me up to date. We agreed to have coffee at eleven at an old haunt of ours near Westminster Bridge.

What he was to tell me was very much of a damper. As far as Wayner's conviction was concerned, it was all cut and dried. He was not only pleading guilty to the Corby

Street job but his counsel would ask for the bank robbery to be taken into account.

"Oh yes, he has a good counsel," Jewle said. "He had to be granted legal aid and Howard Collis was appointed. He's a first-class man, as you know."

I agreed.

"Wayner evidently decided to act on his advice," Jewle went on, "except in one matter. I don't know this for sure, but I'm pretty certain Collis pointed out that if Wayner would disclose the whereabouts of the diamonds there might be a considerable mitigation of sentence. All Wayner did was insist he didn't know a thing about any diamonds. But about that bank job. Wayner knew we had him dead to rights. As for the Corby Street job—well, he was taken in the act. Pleading guilty was the only thing to do, and to hope for some mitigation by owning up to the bank job."

"Tell me something," I said. "Was Wayner ever told he'd been shopped?"

"Not to my knowledge. As you know, we keep that kind of thing well under our hats. Also, except for visits by his counsel, Wayner's been incommunicado."

I said I was sorry to insist but I'd read something in the newspapers.

"Only that something suspicious had been reported," Jewle said. "Certainly not that the place was going to be robbed."

"I see. And now a damn silly question. He hasn't mentioned a confederate?"

"He certainly hasn't. His attitude all along has been that he was caught fair and square and to hell with it. Also he insists he didn't take any diamonds: which, of course, is true. But what's behind all this? What are you trying to get at?"

"I'm trying to work up to it," I told him. "But about Wayner. You saw him. How'd he strike you? I mean personally?"

"To tell the truth, I can't sum him up," he said. "He's a paradox. Good-looking, well-spoken, obviously well-bred. Not a trace of viciousness. That's how Collis feels about him. Says he was the sort who was his own enemy. Came into too much money too soon, ran through it and couldn't lose the spending habit. And maybe got in with the wrong types."

He smiled. "About time I asked a question. What about you people? Nothing interesting turned up?"

"Don't know," I said. "But during the last twenty-four hours I've begun to get the glimmerings of a theory."

He laughed, and I couldn't blame him. He was remembering quite a few years back when we'd both worked under a certain Chief Superintendent to whom any mention by me of a theory was an immediate infuriation. Give me a couple of minutes' notice, he'd bellow, and I could come up with a theory for anything: the vocal chords of Balaam's ass, for instance, or the gullet of the whale that swallowed Jonah.

"Sorry," Jewle said. "You were saying you had an idea."

"It's hardly even that," I said. "You're not in a hurry?"

He told me to carry on, so I mentioned again that matter of the theft of £200 from the safe at The Elms. I gave him an account of my evening with the Morren children: highlighting their knowledge of the bank combination and bringing in the mysterious Scruffy. He was definitely interested.

"Old-fashioned overcoat and a Charlie Chaplin moustache?" he said. "Isn't much to go on. And you think he might have been mixed up in it?"

I didn't want to show too much of my hand. All I wanted was to get the official ball rolling.

"Why did Mrs. Morren lie about him? Also she knew the safe combination. It seems to have been general family knowledge."

"I wouldn't put too much emphasis on that," he said. "After all, there hadn't been a robbery at Corby Street before. It wasn't the sort of thing that had to be specially guarded against. That those diamonds happened to be there was just bad luck. Also how do you explain Wayner?"

"Wayner met all sorts. Scruffy was one of them."

He shook his head. The whole thing was just a bit too much to swallow. He gave a wry smile.

"The trouble with your theories is that sometimes they happen to be right. Anyone else, I'd have laughed them out of court. Not that there's anything we can do except try to unearth this Scruffy. Sure you can't give me any more details?"

I had an idea. A minute or two and the boutique of Helen Cambon was called. He passed a receiver to me and I asked to speak to Miss Greta Morren. The name was Ludovic Travers.

"Good-morning, Mr. Travers." The voice was brightly professional. "I hope you got home safely."

"Indeed, yes," I said. "Even though I kept thinking of someone you told me about. Your friend Scruffy."

She laughed.

"I'm not sure I don't know him," I said. "I run up against all sorts of queer characters, you know. Was he rather tall?"

"Well, in a way, yes. But now I've been thinking. I can tell you who he was really like. You remember the old Laurel and Hardy films? Well, he was like the fat one, only not so fat—if you know what I mean."

That was all I could get. I thanked her, mentioned a probable visit from my wife and rang off. Jewle was looking a bit amused.

"Right," he said. "So I pass the word to pick up Oliver Hardy. If we do, you'd like us to let you know?"

"Just that," I said. "Just where I can find him. After that, we'll see."

That was apparently how we left things, but I knew it wouldn't be quite that way. Jewle never tells more than he thinks expedient, and I had the idea that I'd given him quite a lot to chew on. I was feeling almost pleased with myself by the time I was back at the agency. Then Norris told me John Hill wanted me to ring him.

He'd had the usual interim reports, and now he was asking about prospects. I told him frankly that, as far as the diamonds were concerned, there was little hope of recovery. As for the police, they were of much the same opinion. Even if Wayner's confederate were caught and a case proved, it was still unlikely that the diamonds would be in his possession.

"You haven't asked my opinion," I said, "but I think the claim should be met. There's just one vague idea I'm just about to work on and I'll let you know if anything emerges from it. If not, then I think it's throwing money away to go on employing us. I'm sorry, but that's how I see it."

He said he thought I was right.

The photographers had made a remarkably good job of those rushes. Beryl Morren had been carefully isolated from her daughter and a black-and-white enlargement made. Beryl should be easy enough to identify, and all I had to do was ring Harry Alders and ask if he could spare me a minute or two that afternoon.

It was about three o'clock when I got to Finsbury Park. Harry was in his office. He said I hadn't mentioned what I wanted to see him about, but he guessed it was about Dave.

"You're right," I said. "It's something I've stumbled across. I think he got involved with a woman: older than himself but still very attractive; and it might have been through her he was drawn into that Corby Street business. We've no idea of her name but we do have a photograph. This is it."

He had a long look at it before shaking his head. "Never seen her. Not that I remember."

"Then will you hand these photographs round," I said. "She might have contacted Dave Wayner here: if so, she probably came with a party of friends. Keep the photographs as long as you like. Just send them back as soon as you're satisfied one way or the other."

"Maria," he said. "She's the one most likely to know."

A minute or two and Maria came in. Harry introduced me, but I knew she'd recognised me. She had a long look at the photograph before shaking her head. "I don't know her. Never seen her in my life."

"Just an idea," I said. "We think Dave got involved with this woman."

She gave me a quick look. It was almost a startled look, and for a moment I thought there was something she'd remembered. I was wrong.

"Just hand these round," Harry told her. "Someone might have seen her here. Mr. Travers isn't in any hurry for a day or two."

I asked Harry to do me another favour. I'd never actually seen Dave or even a good photograph. Had he one?

He hadn't one there, he said, but Sandy Scott had one or two. He'd warn him I was on my way up.

The gymnasium was pretty busy. Sandy was standing by the near ring watching a work-out, but he came across as soon as he saw me. As I told him, it was a good many years since I'd seen him in the ring. There was little left of the sandy hair except above the ears, but he looked in good enough condition. He was a cut above what I'd call the ordinary bruiser. I think he'd been an insurance clerk before he'd turned pro. A likeable man: quiet and well-spoken.

We went into his office. The walls were literally lined with souvenir photographs of boxers, only a few of whom I recognised. Dave Wayner's wasn't among them. His were in a drawer of the desk, most of them snapshots taken in the gym. There was a larger one in ordinary clothes. Across the bottom was written in a clear hand—
For Sandy, One of the Best, from Dave.

It was a studio photograph and showed him sitting negligently on the corner of a table, a hand in a trouser pocket and smiling amusedly at the photographer. Everything about him was what I might call normal: he might almost have been an undergraduate of my own day. He was undoubtedly good-looking, and even in that photograph one could discern a something immediately attractive.

"Tell me something, Mr. Scott," I said. "How in heaven's name could a man like this do the things he did?"

Don't ask me, he said. "I don't know. None of us knows. I think it was some kind of disease: you know, after coming into all that money. He got like an alcoholic or a gambler; he just had to have money. Mind you, he always paid his debts. Dave never let anybody down."

"And everybody liked him?"

"Everybody. You couldn't help liking him. There wasn't a thing he wouldn't do for you."

"Yes," I said, "it was a tremendous tragedy. You know the trial's next week?"

He said he'd heard it was shortly. No one at The Carlo would have the heart to go.

"What do you think he'll get?"

I said I didn't know. He might be lucky and get off with three years.

"And what will he do then?"

Again I said I didn't know. Maybe the trustees of his father's will might get him shipped somewhere abroad.

Two days later Harry sent the photographs back. Nobody at The Carlo remembered anyone like Beryl Morren. He added that since our first meeting he'd made some enquiries of his own: no places in particular: just here and there, and he'd heard of no shady characters with whom Dave had been seen.

I rang Jewle and told him my hunch about Beryl Morren seemed to have been wrong. If Dave Wayner had met her it wasn't at The Carlo, and for the moment I could think of no other place where they could have met.

"Bad luck about your man, Scruffy," he said. "Far as I can gather, we've had no dealings with him."

I let John Hill know it would be a waste of time and money for the agency to make further enquiries, and he agreed. All I intended to do, and largely as a matter of curiosity, was to be at the trial.

I did have one other fleeting idea. Wayner's persistent silence had bothered me, and I wondered if the police search of the Corby Street premises had been as thorough as Jewle had insisted, and whether Wayner had had, after all, a chance to secrete those diamonds in some unsuspected place. If so, it would explain his silence. Provided he could recover them when he came out, there would be none too bad a recompense for a spell in jail.

7. END OF AN EPISODE

I WENT to Wayner's trial: not because I expected anything in the nature of a revelation, but mainly to get a look for the first time at Wayner himself. The proceedings themselves took under half an hour. Since the accused was pleading guilty there was no jury to be empanelled. Everything, in fact, was cut and dried.

There were very few of us in court that bitterly cold morning, and most of them were what I'd call the regulars. With a morning off and nothing special to do, I go to Christie's or Sotheby's. It's free; you may learn something, and occasionally it's dramatic. Others get their free entertainment at the criminal courts. In the old days, when I often had to give evidence, I came to recognise quite a few of them by sight.

As I said, the Wayner trial wasn't a *cause célèbre* and it was over in less than no time. Prosecuting counsel outlined his case and was followed by counsel for the defence, who asked that the bank robbery should be taken into account. I missed most of his short plea for mitigation since I was watching Wayner himself.

That photograph I'd seen in Sandy Scott's office had been an excellent one, though his face was much paler than I'd expected. His attitude was quietly observant: he might in some queer way have been merely a spectator like myself. There was a curious unreality about it all which, added to the abnormality of the proceedings themselves, made me feel I was watching not a trial but some strange charade.

Mr. Justice Allman at least was not unexpected. There had to be a homily, but he made it a short one. He could not accept the plea that the accused was the victim of circumstances. What he had done had been deliberately planned and executed, and so on and so on. Then the final remarks, prefixed by a somewhat dramatic *nevertheless*. In the belief that the prisoner might still come to realise the criminal folly of his actions and that the many years ahead of him could still be used to good and proper purpose, the sentence itself would be tempered accordingly. Thereupon he proceeded to sentence David Wayner to a term of four years.

As far as I could see, Wayner didn't move a muscle. There was perhaps just a slight bow before he was taken away, and in some curious way it might have been I who'd been sentenced, not he. All sorts of things flashed through my mind: what Wayner might have been: how The Carlo would take the news: how Wayner himself would take it when he'd had time to think. Four years, I said to myself. With full remission it would be two and two-thirds. I made a quick calculation. By the beginning of October, 1964, Wayner might be released.

I began making my way out. Just ahead of me was a tallish, thick-set man, and as we came out to the pavement he began pulling up round his ears the collar of his dark overcoat. The collar was of some even darker material than the overcoat itself, and then, as he turned, I saw the moustache. I couldn't believe it, and yet it had to be.

I kept at a fairish distance behind him but I needn't have worried. He never once looked back. There was a small queue of us at the Tube station ticket office, but I was near enough to hear him book to Wood Green. When the train came in he took a middle door and I a near one. He'd bought a paper at the station and he began reading it. After that there was no need to give more than an occasional look. At Turnpike Lane he peered out to verify his whereabouts, folded the paper carefully and put it in his pocket. At Wood Green I let him get out ahead of me.

A couple of minutes and he turned into a side street. Almost on the very corner was a shop. A rack of newspapers was outside the door. In one of the windows sweets were on display, and in the other the stock-in-trade of a tobacconist. Immediately beyond was a side passage and through it he disappeared.

I waited a moment or two, then gingerly entered that passage myself. Immediately inside, about head high on the far wall, was a notice:

K. DURFORD
INVESTIGATIONS

An arrow pointed slightly upwards to where a short flight of stairs was clearly visible. I backed out again. That shop was two-storied. Durford apparently rented the premises above. Over the door was:

H. ANSTELL
NEWSAGENT AND TOBACCONIST

I thought of going in, then changed my mind. I walked the few yards back to the main street and then suddenly I thought of a method of approach. Another minute and I was mounting the stairs. A notice on the landing door told me to go straight in.

I went into a tiny waiting-room. It had chairs, two prints—St. Paul's and Buckingham Palace—on the walls, cheapish wall-to-wall carpeting and an electric heater not switched on. A notice painted in black on the frosted window of the door facing me told me to go in. I rapped at the door and did as directed.

It was a cosy little office; more prints on the walls, more carpeting, a couple of spare chairs and an electric fire switched on. There was a small bookcase and a green filing cabinet, and Durford himself in a swivel chair at an old-fashioned, knee-hole mahogany writing desk. His coat and hat were on a stand by another door to my right.

He'd glanced up as I'd entered. He got to his feet.

"Mr. Durford?"

"Yes, sir. At your service. Will you take a chair?"

There was indeed the faintest look of Oliver Hardy. The voice had no particular accent.

"And now, sir, what can I do for you?"

He was giving me a pretty shrewd look. I doubted if I was the kind who usually entered that office.

"It's rather involved," I said. "My name's Travers, by the way: Ludovic Travers."

He moistened his lips. "Wait a minute, sir. The name seems familiar."

He remembered quite a lot as soon as I told him just who I was.

"I've heard a lot about that organisation of yours," he said, and smiled deprecatingly. "What I run is only a one-man affair."

"Why not?" I said. "We all have to live. Don't think me rude, but you seem to be doing reasonably well."

"I manage," he said. "A fair number of jobs. Some good, some not so good. You know how it is. Also one or two agencies get me to lend a hand from time to time." He leaned slightly forward. "Was that what you wanted to see me about?"

"As a matter of fact, no," I said. "I don't say an opportunity mightn't arise in the future, but what interested me was the fact that you were at the Wayner trial this morning."

He stared. "You mean you followed me here?"

I told him he could put it that way. He shook his head.

"I must be losing my touch. But why? Why should it be important to you?"

I told him exactly why the agency was interested.

"And there were you, an enquiry agent like myself—"

"Just a minute, sir. You knew me?"

"One gets around," I said. "If I hadn't known who you were, would I be here? Much more comfortable than talking on the street. In any case, I asked myself why you were so far from home for the sake of a cut-and-dried case like the Wayner one. In other words, I thought I'd like to lay some cards on the table. Mind if I ask you a question or two?"

He leaned back in the chair. "Why not, sir?"

"Then did you actually know Wayner?"

"Never met him in my life. Never clapped eyes on him till this morning."

"Did you know Morren, the head of the Corby Street firm Wayner stole the diamonds from?"

"Never heard the name till I saw it in the papers."

"Then we're left with one thing," I said. "You were interested, as I was, in the recovery of the diamonds."

"Could be," he said. "That reward they're offering wouldn't do me any harm."

He smiled. His head went slightly sideways. "I think I get it. You think I have some ideas. For which, perhaps, you'd be prepared to pay?"

"To put it bluntly, yes."

He thought it over for a moment. He began hoisting his ample body from the chair. I wondered for a moment if he was about to kick me out.

"I don't know about yourself, sir, but I feel like a cup of coffee. Can I make one for you?"

He left the door ajar and I could hear him pottering around. In a very short time he was back with a couple of steaming cups, and a sugar bowl, on a tray.

"A very comfortable place you have here, Mr. Durford."

"I was lucky," he said. "Used to be in the police before the war, then I joined up. Stayed on for a ten-year term and when I came out I worked for a time with London Enquiries. That was when Larry Farman had it. You knew him?"

I said I'd heard of him.

"Then my daughter married Harold Anstell who owned the shop, and as they didn't want the upstairs rooms they let me have them when I thought of going into the profession for myself."

"A very lucky arrangement," I told him. "But to get back to that diamond business. Any ideas to offer us?"

I'd thought that offer of coffee had been an excuse to think things over. At any rate, he came up with an idea.

"To tell the truth, sir, I don't think I've got anything you haven't got yourselves. All the same, I don't know how it struck you this morning, but I thought Wayner took it all a bit too calmly."

He gave me a questioning look.

"And so?"

"Well, if he has those diamonds, or knows where they are, he could afford to."

"Yes," I said. "I thought so too. What about a confederate?"

"That's another thing. There wasn't any mention of one. Also, the papers seemed to play the whole thing down. I've known a smash-and-grab get more publicity."

"That was because it was almost cut and dried," I said. "Wayner was caught red-handed. You knew he was shopped?"

He stared.

"Keep it strictly to yourself, but the police had a tip-off. That's why Wayner was picked up almost as soon as he entered the place."

He shook his head. "Seems queer to me the police didn't let it out. It couldn't have done any harm."

"They have their methods and we have ours," I said. "But about yourself. You just turned up this morning on the off chance?"

"That's right. Five hundred quid is five hundred quid. You never know."

"Well, that's that," I said, and began getting to my feet. "If you run across anything you feel you can't handle yourself or you'd prefer to pass on, just give me a ring."

I thanked him for the coffee and told him the next time we found ourselves short-handed I'd get in touch. His terms seemed very reasonable. He accompanied me out and down the stairs to the street, but when I looked back at the main road he had gone.

I made for Fleet Street and the offices of the *Sunday Record*. In the previous Sunday's edition I found Durford's name among the classified ads.

K. DURFORD—investigations. Secrecy guaranteed.

Just that, plus the address and the telephone number. There were a dozen almost similar notices in that section, and only two mentioned absolute secrecy. The rest were either saving money or taking their good faith as understood. All, like Durford, had no fixed clientele. It was advertisements that brought the clients. Not that there was anything derogatory about that.

At the agency I checked the Association list to see if Durford was a member. He wasn't. Not again that there was anything very wrong about that. Next I rang London Enquiries and asked to speak to Fred Halsey. He used to be one of their operatives but now has an office job.

"I remember him," he said. "Must be two or three years now since he did anything for us. You've got something in mind for him?"

"Maybe," I said. "Just wanted a confidential opinion."

"He's reliable enough," Fred said. "Any run-of-the-mill job'll suit him."

That was about all. Then I tried to get hold of Jewle. He wasn't available, and it wasn't till late that afternoon that I finally got him. If he could spare me ten minutes I'd be grateful. He told me to come along. I rang off before he could ask me what it was all about.

Calling at the Yard on the way home meant only a slight detour. There'd seemed too much to say over the telephone, and a talk in Jewle's room suited me fine. As it happened, it didn't take all that long.

"A stroke of luck, as you say," he said. "You sure this Durford is the right man?"

I said I was sure. What I wasn't sure about was the man himself. He seemed a solid enough character. He had highly respectable premises and was apparently getting a reasonable living. Also he'd made no bones about giving me a brief biography.

Jewle said that was something that could be checked, so I wrote down everything I could remember.

"Just the two things against him," I said. "There's the fact that he was sufficiently interested to be at that trial this morning. And that he told at least one lie when he said he'd never even heard the name Morren."

"That's something we can't check," Jewle said. "Even if we took the risk of asking what he did for Mrs. Morren, he'd be entitled to keep his mouth shut. You ought to know that. It isn't as if we were dealing with anything like murder. As for being where he was this morning—well, the reason he gave you might be valid. He thought there might be a chance to pick something up that'd give him a try for that £500."

That was about all. He said he'd do what he could and let me know. It shouldn't take more than two or three days. And three days later it was. He rang me just as Bertha was about to bring in morning coffee.

"About your friend," he said. "Everything's been checked and everything's in order. His record's absolutely what he said it was. Also we've never had any reason whatever to get into contact with him since he opened that office."

"You don't think he could have told me what he did as a sort of blind? Knowing it might be checked?"

He laughed. "You certainly don't let go. But look: take my advice. Everything's over. Just let it rest—till the time comes."

My laugh was more of a snort. "And when'll that be?"

"When Wayner comes out," he said. "If he did have a confederate and that confederate still has the diamonds, then Wayner'll contact him. That's all I can suggest."

I told him he was probably right, thanked him for letting me be so much of a nuisance, and rang off. And there I really did intend to let things rest. After all, I could piously assure myself that we at the agency had done all we could, and that, without the gratuitous help of Jewle, we'd have done considerably less. So I got hold of John

Hill, told him that hunch I'd had had produced nothing, gave him Jewle's considered opinion and waited to hear what he'd say. He agreed entirely with Jewle.

But even then I couldn't let the matter rest. I have an insatiable curiosity and I hate an unsolved mystery. I just had to go on grubbing about till even I was convinced that Jewle had been right. Also it so happened that there was nothing at the moment to tie me to the office, so, for one thing, I went down to Insbury and did some probing into that bank robbery. I read the local paper and even got permission to see the police file. It was a waste of time. Nothing emerged that I didn't already know.

I rang Corby Street, hoping to speak to Morren, but he was away on a valuation. It seemed an excellent chance to see the staff, and George Ward seemed pleased to have me pay a call.

It was as interesting an hour as I'd had for a long time. Those two presentation caskets were almost finished, and it was fascinating to watch a couple of experts at work.

"One thing puzzles me," I said to Ward. "When you have valuable things like these, what do you do with them at night? Surely you don't keep them in the safe?"

"These are only valuable from what I might call our point of view," he told me. "To a thief they'd just be silver to be melted down. All the same, they'll go to the local bank. Anything of real value is always deposited just before it closes. It doesn't affect us. We've nearly always got something else to carry on with."

"Then what could a burglar find in the safe?"

He shrugged his shoulders.

"Just oddments. Metal clippings, or sweepings. Perhaps a few inferior stones. Nothing that wouldn't be covered by the standing insurance."

I must have frowned.

"You're wondering about the diamonds." Ward said. "I've wondered about that too. Know what we think? And that includes the boss. It was a special occasion, for one thing. Also he definitely intended to go back upstairs and take the diamonds with him, then it slipped his mind."

I said it was understandable. And, after all, there hadn't been a burglary in the whole history of the firm. All the same, I couldn't help thinking that it couldn't have been entirely chance that on that one night £10,000 worth of diamonds had happened to be in that safe. For the rest, I was disposed to agree with Jewle. To suspect any of Morren's staff was virtually unthinkable.

You might say that that visit to Corby Street brought me to the end of my tether. Even I had to admit that the case was closed. We always keep our files for at least ten years. I saw that this particular one was absolutely up to date before consigning it to the special cabinet. I discarded only one thing—those rush photographs of Beryl Morren. They were never likely to be wanted again. And I did have that coloured original.

I had a last look at it before clipping it into the file. It brought back quite a lot of memories: my first sight of her, for instance, and the wonder if it had really been she who had taken that £200. Then there'd been that evening with Lorenz Brander and later with the Morren children at Flagon Street. I remembered I'd never asked Bernard Morren to lunch and I wondered if I'd given

Bernice a cheque for that twin-set she'd bought at the Maison Cambon.

And that, as they say, was that. The file was put away and, unconscionable a time though it had been a-dying, it was now as good as dead. If John Hill should happen to want further action taken when Wayner came out of jail, he'd have only to ring. But that wouldn't be till almost three years' time, which, as things go these days, looked quite a distance away.

PART II: THE RELEASE

8. OVERTURE

ONE morning towards the end of that September Norris referred me to an entry in the diary, special for that year. It was a reminder about the release of David Wayner.

That afternoon I managed to get hold of Jewle. He said he'd get the exact date for me and give me a ring.

"Any method of finding out who his visitors were—if he had any?"

"Why?"

"Just trying to get in touch with things again," I said. "That business of a confederate happened to come into my mind."

"It's possible," he said. "But he hasn't been in the same little cell all the time."

He said he might be round my way in the morning and that's how we left it. I postponed my usual coffee time, but not for long. He turned up shortly before eleven. I hadn't seen him since his holiday and I told him he was looking extraordinarily fit. I don't have a set holiday. What I like is a week here and another there, depending on the pressure of work. It means you've always something to look forward to, and it breaks up the year.

When we got round to David Wayner, he hadn't much for me, except that the date of release was the 2nd of October at around ten o'clock. As for visitors, he'd consistently refused to see any.

"I think you were oversimplifying things," Jewle told me. "Considering the circumstances, a confederate would never risk a visit. If any information had to be got through to Wayner, it could be done in a letter. Letters are censored, as you know, but it isn't the job of prison authorities to hunt for clues to the whereabouts of stolen property. If it comes to that, it isn't our job either—not in this case. Everything was too hypothetical. The existence of a confederate was never actually proved. You were at Wayner's trial, so you know it wasn't even mentioned."

That was about all he could tell me, except that Wayner had been a model prisoner. For the last twelve months he'd actually been working in the prison library. As for the definite time of release, Jewle said he'd give me a confirmatory ring the day before.

The next day John Hill rang me. His attention had just been called to the fact that Wayner was about to be released. I asked if he wished the case to be reopened.

"That's what I'd like your opinion about," he said. "As I see it, there'd surely be no harm in keeping him under observation for a few days. After all, there was a possibility of a confederate."

"We'll do just that," I said. "Nothing elaborate. Just try to find out where he goes and what his contacts are. No use throwing a lot of good money after bad."

That's how we left it. That's one of the good things about John Hill—he doesn't keep a dog and bark himself. He may give a little whimper from time to time, but that's hardly the same thing.

I got the old Morren file out of the cabinet and began having a look through it. Under three years since I'd last seen it and yet somehow it was something out of almost a primordial past. I had to do quite a lot of thinking back in order to get myself once more in touch with things.

And even after a few minutes' hard thinking I had the feeling that I still wasn't near enough to the case. And then I had an idea. It was getting on for midday, so I took a bus to Piccadilly Circus. It was a lovely day. The morning had had an autumnal mist and, now it had cleared, the sun was almost hot.

I walked along Regent Street and turned down Flagon Street. The offices of London Publications were only a few doors along. I asked to see Mr. Morren. A couple of minutes and the girl at Enquiries was telling me that he'd be down very shortly. I pottered around in the main hall, looking at books on display till he appeared.

It seems rather ridiculous now to say that he looked older. He certainly looked more mature, but I'd certainly have known him anywhere. And he as certainly recognised me. He gave quite a pleasant smile as he held out his hand.

"Mr. Travers, isn't it?"

"It is," I said. "And a rather guilty one. How are you, Bernard?"

He said he was fine. I said I was too.

"Just happened to be this way, and I suddenly remembered something. Almost three years ago I was going to ask you to have lunch with me at my club."

He laughed. "No need to apologise. As a matter of fact I'd forgotten all about it myself."

"But what about this morning?" I said. "You're free?"

"That's most kind of you," he said.

He had quite an attractive smile. "As a matter of fact we have quite a nice canteen here which we're expected to patronise, but it does get a bit dull. Shall we go along to my office?"

We went upstairs to a pleasant-looking room. While he cleared up some oddments of business I rang the club and booked a table for two. Ten minutes later I was hailing a taxi in Regent Street.

"And how're things shaping with you?" I said.

"Pretty good," he said. "I'm in the editorial department at the moment. Quite interesting work."

"And that book you were writing? The thriller."

"Heavens!" he said. "Fancy you remembering that!"

I said I'd kept a kind of touch because I had an eye out for its appearance. He shook his head a bit ruefully.

"To be perfectly frank, it's still only half-written. The more I learn about publishing, the less I think of myself as an author—even of thrillers."

"Plenty of time yet," I said. "By the way, I hope you didn't mind my calling you Bernard. After all, I'm old enough to be your father."

"Please don't apologise," he said. "I like it. But tell me about yourself. How are things in the insurance business?"

I managed to spin out the conversation till we got to the club. Inside he seemed very impressed. I told him, over a pre-prandial sherry, that it was about time he became a member. As a Cambridge man of, I hoped, unblemished reputation, he was qualified.

"Think it over," I said. "It'd be an excellent thing for a young fellow like you. A handy place to bring clients to and to take refuge in yourself. Plenty of useful contacts once you were known."

He seemed inordinately grateful. Mind you, it wasn't wholly a scattering of seed. I liked young Morren and I meant all I said. Luckily, too, there was an excellent menu that day. At times a club lunch can be a bit too homely, but he was describing the curried turbot as excellent, and I was getting on well with some fried chicken.

"I was just recalling that evening at your apartment," I said. "You still live there?"

"Oh yes. I'm very lucky really. It's so handy. A bit solitary at times now Greta's gone. You remember my sister?"

"Indeed, yes."

"She used to make it a kind of *pied-à-terre*. Then she married Frank Sievers. You remember him. He was with us that night."

"Remember him very well," I said. "When I was at your place that evening I think they were only engaged."

"Greta was always potty about Frank," he said. "She hadn't known him more than a week before she was telling me she was going to marry him."

"A happy marriage, then?"

He smiled. "Almost sickeningly so, if you know what I mean. But I like Frank. He's an awfully decent chap.

Plenty of money too, which helps. By the way, they have a small daughter. Born last March."

"Which makes you an uncle. You see them often?"

"Only occasionally. They have quite a nice place at Northwood."

"And she's still with that—what was its name?"

"Helen Cambon. Oh no. Frank insisted she drop all that after they were married. Also they were in Paris for some months. His firm were opening a branch there."

He had the plum tart by way of dessert. I had cheese.

"And your uncle?" I said. "You've seen him recently?"

"About three weeks ago. He hasn't altered a lot."

I smiled. "Let me do some calculating. This year it was again the turn of the family to dine with him at his hotel."

"No," he said. "It wasn't like that. Just that things were a bit different."

I didn't press the point. His look had suddenly been so serious that it would have been the worst of manners to probe any deeper. But, in a way, I was to be lucky. We had coffee and a liqueur in the smaller reading-room, and it was there that he reopened things.

"You met my father, of course, but did you ever meet my mother?"

I told him the circumstances under which I'd met them both.

"That was a queer business," he said. "As far as I know, it never was cleared up. But about my parents. You didn't know they'd separated?"

"I'd no idea."

"Yes," he said. "It wasn't very long after that diamond robbery. Not that Greta and I hadn't expected something like it. Things had been getting a bit sticky, if you know what I mean. At any rate, Mother got a divorce. Just after Greta married Frank. Not long afterwards she got married again. To Arthur Lambourn. You've heard of him?"

I hadn't.

"He owns, among other things, a gaming club near Knightsbridge. They've a very nice place at West Hampstead. Mind you, he's a very nice fellow. I like him. He and Mother get along fine. So I believe. I don't see a lot of them."

"And your father? He still lives at Cockfosters?"

"Yes," he said. "But there was an awful tragedy there. He's all alone there now, except for the servants. The same married couple we had when you were there."

I had to hear more about that tragedy. It hadn't sounded as if it was merely that matter of the divorce.

"I liked your father," I said. "I hope it was nothing serious that happened."

"It was," he said. "From his point of view, I mean. It didn't affect Greta and me so much. You see, it was like this. After the divorce he got married again too. She was much younger than he and quite good-looking, and all that, but we—I mean Greta and me—we didn't like her. We thought there was something just a bit cheap about her. Then it turned out later on that she'd been a model for a Birmingham firm. I'm sorry to sound so snobbish, but that's how it was."

"You still go to Cockfosters occasionally?"

He shook his head. "I'm afraid I didn't tell you everything. Pamela—that was our new stepmother—was killed about six months ago. In a motor accident. Killed instantaneously. In one of those pile-ups on the M-1."

"Terrible," I said. "Your father's certainly had a pretty rotten time."

"Yes," he said. "He's got a lot older. Greta and I see him as often as we can. Sometimes we manage to have lunch together in town. He loves his grand-daughter. That's the one good thing that's happened to him."

"Don't say the business has gone wrong too?"

He looked surprised. "Heavens no! I believe he's doing very well."

A few minutes later our taxi dropped him at the entrance to Flagon Street. He seemed extraordinarily grateful for that time he'd spent with me, and I told him as we shook hands that he must think about the club and let me know when he'd made his mind up. He'd grown into a really nice boy. It was a long while since I'd taken to anyone so quickly and so much.

I took a bus from Piccadilly back to Broad Street, and I kept going over and over again the various happenings he'd told me. Under three years. I said to myself, and in just one family there'd been incredible changes. Something had been very wrong with my thinking. Because I myself had been standing somewhat still and merely growing older in a revolving world, I'd imagined I'd be picking up the threads of the Morren case not far from the point where they'd been left. Not that those changes could affect David Wayner. He would have undergone his own changes, and he too, like myself that morning, would have threads to pick up in that private world of his which had been unknown to even Harry Alders: the world of shady characters and expensive tastes: the world where he had heard of a safe in Corby Street. And—the question came suddenly out of nowhere—that on a certain night that safe would contain diamonds to the value of ten thousand pounds?

9. ON THE TRAIL

THE day before Wayner was due for release Jewle rang to confirm the time. I rang Harry Alders and asked if he could spare me a minute.

I found him, as usual, in his office, and I put the question to him straight away. Did he know that Dave Wayner was being released the next morning?

"I had a rough idea," he said. "Dave wrote me just about a fortnight ago."

"You've corresponded regularly?"

"Oh no," he said. "The first letter I wrote he didn't answer. Then I wrote him another when he was at Penstone. All he said was there was nothing he wanted and he didn't want to see anybody. So I left it like that. Then he wrote about a fortnight ago, as I said. Asked me to have all his things packed up for him." He pointed to the corner. "That's them there, in those two cases."

That was good news, though Harry didn't know it. Also there was something I wanted from him, so I handed out some information. Dave Wayner might have those diamonds, or know where to lay his hands on them. If the police caught him in possession, it might mean a new charge. The old one had been entering with intent, so it was better that we picked him up in possession rather than the police. I made it a bit wordy and obscure, but he got the general drift.

"Since he got you to have his belongings ready, it's almost a certainty that he'll come straight here," I said. "What we'd like you to do is make sure. Meet him yourself with a car. Could you do that?"

He thought it over. Finally he said he could be there but it was no guarantee that Dave would accept a ride. I said he'd be doing us a great favour and Dave, perhaps, an even bigger one, and that was how we left it. He'd be near the prison gates a few minutes before ten.

It certainly simplified things for the agency. Hallows would be waiting too. If Wayner accepted the ride, then he was to get to Finsbury Park as soon as he could. If Wayner refused the ride, then Hallows would follow him. I was to go straight to Finsbury Park in my car and wait somewhere near till I made a contact.

It was a lovely morning of early October; the sun shining and the air fresh and bracing. Hallows would be going direct to the prison from his home: I went, as agreed, to Finsbury Park. I found a parking place in a little side street not a hundred yards from The Carlo. Wayner didn't know either me or Hallows, so it didn't matter if we were seen.

Hallows joined me near The Carlo just before eleven. He said he'd seen Wayner and Harry having a talk on the pavement not far from the prison. Harry had probably been persuading him to get in the car, which was what Wayner finally did.

"One thing I didn't like," Hallows said. "Almost as soon as Harry's big Humber moved off again, a taxi drew in not far behind it. I couldn't see who the passenger was but it kept nicely behind all along Farnham Street, and when the Humber turned right into Raleigh Terrace it turned in too. Might have been someone following Wayner, or it mightn't."

If someone's taxi had really been following Wayner, then it would almost certainly go the whole way. The trouble was our plans had been made and they didn't involve a split-up. All we could do was stay put and hope for the best.

It was just after half-past eleven when Harry's car drew in at the small parking place at the south end of The Carlo. Harry got out first and Wayner followed him through a side door which would be at the far end of the bowling alley. All we could see of Wayner was that he was wearing a dark felt hat and a dark three-quarter-length coat with an imitation fur collar: the clothes he'd doubtless been wearing that night in Corby Street.

Hallows fetched our car and we sat there for about twenty minutes with the main entrance of The Carlo in view. Then an empty taxi drew up. The driver waited for a minute or two, then sounded his horn. Almost at once Wayner came out. Behind him a man—a waiter probably—was carrying the couple of medium-sized suitcases. Wayner himself had been carrying a smaller one. A second or two and the taxi moved off. The waiter watched it for a moment or two, then went back inside the building. Hallows moved his car off behind the taxi. I waited for a bit and then went in myself. Harry was in his office, as I'd expected.

"You made it then?" I said.

"Yes," he said, "but it wasn't too easy. Then I told him it was all for his convenience and it wasn't costing anything, so he got in."

"Did he talk?"

"Hardly at all. Before he got in the car I made everything clear, how there was no place for him now at The Carlo. He said he knew it. Then after we got started I had to watch the traffic, and I don't suppose we said more than a dozen words the whole way."

"And what about when he got in here?"

"Well, he asked if he could go through his things and could I find him a smaller suitcase. Far as I could see, he wanted it for his toilet things and so on; so what I thought was that he had somewhere in mind for the night and was going to park the rest somewhere else."

"You're probably right." I said. "And how did he strike you in himself?"

"I didn't like it. He was too quiet. Never a smile, never a friendly word—nothing. You know what he looked like? Someone who's just going into the ring to fight a man he hates the bloody sight of. I tell you, Mr. Travers, if I hadn't known I could handle him I'd have been scared."

I said I thought I knew. That spell in jail, for a man like Wayner, must have been hell. It had left its marks.

"What about his intentions? Did he tell you anything?"

"Nothing at all. Only that I wasn't to worry. He'd get along fine."

"What about money? Did he have any?"

Harry looked the least bit sheepish.

"To tell you the truth, I gave him something. Only a tenner. That was the only time he was anything like his old self. He said, 'Thank you, Harry. I shan't forget it,' or something like that. Then we shook hands and that was it. I hoped he might have asked about Sandy, but he didn't.

Never a word about anybody. All he did was to ask me to order a taxi and get someone to carry the cases out."

I thanked him for his co-operation and then I went back to the agency, hoping there might be some news from Hallows. I was just about to ask Bertha to fetch me some sandwiches when Hallows came on the line.

"Something's happened," he said. "Can't explain now, but can you come to Charing Cross station straight away? I'll be by the bookstall."

Traffic would be bad, even at midday, so I took a District train from The Monument. Hallows was waiting by the bookstall at Charing Cross.

"I've lost him," he said, just like that.

He began telling me about it. The trip had been uneventful and there'd been no difficulty about keeping Wayner's taxi in sight. The trouble came when it was obvious that the taxi was about to turn into the station court, since there was nowhere handy for himself to park. What he'd done was take a chance and move with the petering traffic into Northumberland Avenue and leave the car there.

He said he'd almost sprinted back to the station and he was in luck. Wayner was checking the two larger suitcases in at the left-luggage office. Then, carrying the smaller case, he went to the bookstall and bought a paper.

"That's when I lost him," Hallows said. "He went along there and through the hotel doors. He didn't look round and he didn't hurry, and as soon as I saw him go through I told myself he was going to treat himself to a posh lunch, so I let him get well inside. I took a quick look in the dining-room but he wasn't there, so I guessed he'd be having a wash and brush-up. But he wasn't. He wasn't even in one of the lavatories. I nipped back to the dining-room and asked a waiter if he'd seen him, and he hadn't. Then I wondered if he'd gone straight through to the station yard door, so I had a look round. I even took a look along both ways outside. Then I rang you."

I asked him how much time he reckoned Wayner had had from the moment he'd gone through the hotel doors. He thought it had been at least five minutes.

That he might by then be heaven knew where was, for the moment, less important than the knowledge that he'd been deliberately trying to disappear. He couldn't have been aware that Hallows had followed him, so whom was he trying to avoid? Or was it that he wanted to be absolutely sure of secrecy when the time came to make a contact?

"It's the very devil," Hallows said. "If he *is* going to make contact with someone, it might be almost at once. Everything's gone down the drain."

"Maybe," I said. "But we still have one contact with him ourselves—the luggage. Sooner or later he'll collect it—"

I stopped short.

"Or will it be a long time later? He took care to put everything he might need in the bag he was carrying. It'll rank as luggage at any hotel in town. I don't know if he had any money of his own, but the tenner Harry Alders gave him ought to last him three or four days."

"Wait a minute," Hallows said. "I'm not so sure the luggage is still there. Let's go and see."

There were two attendants there and he waited till the older man was free. He showed him his agency warrant card. It is as like the police card as makes no difference, and just enough unlike to keep us out of trouble.

"A youngish man wearing a dark felt hat and a dark jacket left two cases here about ten minutes ago. Are they still here?"

"Oh, them," he said. "They went out almost as soon as they came in."

"But he couldn't have collected them himself. I'd have seen him."

The man smiled. "I know he didn't. It was a porter who fetched them. He gave me the ticket and I gave him the two cases. His name's Walsh. Fellow about my own age. Shortish. If I was you I'd ask outside."

We went out. A likely-looking porter was putting some luggage into a taxi that had just drawn up. The moment he was free Hallows worked the warrant-card trick.

"You're Mr. Walsh?"

He was. He told us just what had happened. Wayner had given him the ticket and asked him to fetch two suitcases while he grabbed an incoming taxi.

"That's all that happened. When I came back he had a taxi and I gave the driver the bags. The gent gave me half a crown."

"You know who the driver was?"

He knew him by sight but not by name. Hallows took out a pound note.

"Ask around. Someone might know. We'd like his name. If not, where he works from. Try and make it snappy. You'll find us in the main refreshment room."

We weren't too happy over the coffee and sandwiches. There'd been something too organised about it all. Except for getting that ride in Harry Alders's car, Wayner had had the whole thing planned. It had had a speed and a slickness which, as Hallows admitted, had left him flat-footed. And the vital question for us was just why?

It must have been far more than a wish to retire into some new, private world, well away from his pre-prison haunts and acquaintances round, say, Finsbury Park. He could have done that in a perfectly normal way without any of the cloak-and-dagger stuff. In fact, the only thing that made sense was inherent in the very reason why we ourselves were there: with the hope—admittedly a faint one—that Wayner would make contact with someone who had the Morren diamonds or the proceeds of their sale. Wayner's carefully planned disappearance made our reasons suddenly more valid: the ironic outcome had been that Wayner could now make contact at his leisure, with no hope of our finding him till it was far too late.

We'd just about finished the snack when Walsh looked through the door. We joined him.

"Think I've got what you wanted," he told Hallows. "His name's Packer and he works for the City Hire Company. Just off Cannon Street."

Hallows gave him another note. We collected Hallows' car and made for Cannon Street. It wouldn't be a two-man job, so I got out just short and went on to the agency. Hallows would ring me if I were needed.

He didn't ring me. He turned up himself about half an hour later. Nothing could be known till Packer reported in, which ought to be around five o'clock. He'd arranged with the firm to ring us as soon as anything was known.

It was a pretty restless afternoon. What we had to face was the likelihood that we might never clap eyes on Wayner again. If a meeting with his Corby Street confederate was the reason—and we could think of no other—for throwing any possible trailers off the scent, then Wayner might already have seen that confederate and collected his share of the proceeds. Even considering the price that would have been paid by the fence, Wayner would have in his pocket enough to take him almost anywhere on earth.

Five o'clock came and it wasn't long afterwards that the City Hire Company rang. Their man had taken the fare to Baker Street Station. The last that had been seen of him was standing with the luggage on the pavement near the main entrance.

There was nothing for it but to make for Baker Street. It seemed pretty futile. If Wayner had been intending to make a thorough job of it, he'd have hailed a taxi at Baker Street and gone on with the merry-go-round, and this time we'd have no chance at all of finding the taxi. Jewle might do it perhaps, but even he might take anything up to a couple of days: which, as Euclid would have said, was absurd. The only way to get any information about the diamonds was to find Wayner before contact with the confederate had been made, and for that we might already be too late.

But we had to give it a try. No point whatever in trying to trace another taxi. Our hope was that Wayner might have deposited his luggage. If he had, and it was still there, then sooner or later he'd have to collect it.

We tried the left-luggage office and struck lucky. At about half-past one two cases had been left by a man of Wayner's description. Half an hour later they'd been collected by the same man. When he'd left them originally he'd been carrying three cases—a smaller one tucked against an arm; when he'd collected the two cases he hadn't the small case with him.

We adjourned to the refreshment room to talk things over. The answer to the riddle of the three cases seemed to be this, that, carrying the one case, Wayner had disappeared for half an hour. What he'd been looking for was quite unknown, but the chances were that it was a hotel. Having found one, he'd booked in and then returned for the rest of his luggage. If he'd carried the reasonably heavy bags there himself, that surely made the hotel not too far away.

"Something doesn't fit," Hallows said. "Or does it? From the moment he left Finsbury Park he was really making for here. Why here? If it was because of a hotel, then it must have been one he'd had in mind all along. One he'd once stayed at, say: so mightn't there be the chance of being recognised?"

"It might have been years ago," I said. "Also Wayner wasn't a notorious character whose face everyone would be likely to know. And he'd have booked in under another name."

There was only one thing for it, to get a list of all the hotels in the immediate neighbourhood. At the information bureau we were given a list of all London hotels, and we had to adjourn to a waiting-room to sort out the Baker Street area for ourselves. It was amazing the number we found. Within half-a-mile radius, approximately, we found no fewer than twenty.

It was after six o'clock. I suggested leaving it till the morning, when we could use an extra man.

"I'd like to have a crack at it straight away," Hallows said. "After all, it was I who got us into this mess."

I told him not to be damn silly. He'd nothing to reproach himself with. It had just been one of those things.

"And something else," I said. "If Wayner went on being as smart as he had been, then he'd have found means to change his appearance. I doubt if he'd have been wearing that hat and jacket, for instance. So how're you going to describe him at an hotel?"

He was obstinate. He said he'd take a chance; so, since he had that bee in his bonnet, there wasn't any point in hunting for something else to put him off. I said I'd get along home and if he had any news he could ring me there. I'd get hold of Norris and ask him to have a man on call first thing in the morning, just in case.

It was about nine o'clock when Hallows rang me. He was calling it a day. He'd tried five hotels on the south side and had had no luck. Maybe things would go better in the morning. I didn't say so but I wasn't so sure. Even hotels were pure hypothesis. In spite of the fact that Wayner hadn't been carrying the small case when he'd collected the larger cases, he still might have taken a taxi. The taxi-driver, for instance, might have been holding the small case while Wayner collected the others.

During the night there was a change of weather: no sun at all and a thin drizzle in the air. It wasn't the weather for optimism, even if I did get to the agency well before my usual time. Hallows had got there earlier still. French, one of our best operatives, was with him.

We got to work at once. French was put as far as was strictly necessary into the picture and we worked out the exact location of the remaining hotels. Hallows said there'd be no need for me to go. If anything was unearthed, I'd be rung, and decisions could be made. It seemed a sensible sort of arrangement to me.

It was just after nine o'clock when they left. There was nothing much for me to do, so I just sat around. Till just before ten o'clock, when Bertha buzzed through to say that Jewle was on the line.

"Glad you were in," he said. "You're busy?"

Something suddenly told me it might pay to put him in the picture: not too far in: just enough to get him interested in case we might want his help. So I told him about our day with Wayner. I'd hardly begun when he was giving a chuckle.

"So you came round to the confederate idea after all!"

I said we had to take everything into account and went on to give him an edited edition of the rest. He seemed interested.

"You might be working on the right lines," he said. "Thanks for telling me, but I was ringing you about something else. Didn't you know Morren's son? I think you told me you'd run across him."

"I know him pretty well," I said. "Only a few days ago he had lunch with me."

"Then you probably know where he lives," he said. "Could you meet me in Flagon Street in, say, half an hour?"

10. THE BURGLAR

BEFORE I'd had time to ask Jewle what had happened to Bernard Morren he'd rung off. What had actually happened I couldn't imagine, but if Jewle himself was now concerned it had to be pretty serious. As I've said, I liked young Morren and I wasn't feeling too happy as I set out for Flagon Street.

*

Jewle's car was drawn up outside No. 97. He came a few yards to meet me. He said there was a place a little farther on where we could get a cup of coffee and have a minute or two's chat. I asked him straight out what had happened to Bernard Morren.

"Nothing too serious," he said. "To tell the truth. I'm still not sure I should have asked you to come along. Just by luck one of my sergeants happened to mention the name Morren in an overnight report and—well, that's how it started. You'll have to judge for yourself."

As soon as we got settled down to the coffee he told me what had happened. At about seven o'clock the previous night a call had been received at the Yard. A disturbance was going on, like people fighting, so a squad car was rushed in. In the apartment above the bookshop they found Bernard Morren unconscious. He'd been badly knocked about: mouth cut, and, as was discovered when the doctor arrived, two broken ribs. When he came to, which was almost at once, he said he'd got home just before seven and had found a burglar in the apartment. He'd tried to collar him, there'd been a struggle but the man had escaped.

"I know," Jewle said. "You're going to say what's unusual about that, so I'll tell you. Or, better still, you can see and hear everything and make your own mind up. But tell me what you know about this Bernard Morren."

I told him I'd met him on only two occasions, but I thought I knew him pretty well. The brief biography didn't take more than a couple of minutes.

"So you saw the flat." Jewle said. "Anything there to tempt a burglar?"

"Depends on the class of burglar," I said. "There was a radiogram and a television set and a cocktail cabinet, all high-class. Might possibly have been some money. I don't know."

"Yes," Jewle said. "As you say, it depended on the class of burglar. He might have made an entry just on the off-chance. The fact that the shop was closed might have been a temptation."

He paid the small bill and we went back. I stood behind him on the landing while he pushed the bell. Almost at once the door opened.

"Yes?" a woman's voice said.

Jewle introduced himself. He was told to go in. I followed. I gave a little start of surprise.

"Greta, isn't it? Sorry. Mrs. Sievers. Bernard told me."

"And you're Mr. Travers. You were here that evening after we'd been with Uncle Lorenz. You gave us all a lift."

"A long time ago," I said. "But I had lunch with Bernard only the other day."

"I know," she said. "He told me."

She was giving Jewle an enquiring look.

"Mr. Travers had mentioned your brother," he said, "so I let him know about what happened last night. I was coming this way in any case. How is your brother?"

"Quite comfortable now," she said. "As soon as the doctor told him last night he'd have to spend a few days in bed he got him to ring me, and I came along to look after him. There wasn't anyone else—not really."

She didn't look much different from when I'd last seen her. A bit more mature, perhaps, but just as attractive.

"You think we could see your brother?" Jewle said.

"I'm sure you can," she said. "Perhaps I'd better have a look at him first."

She went into the bedroom and we waited. I had a look round the room. Nothing seemed to have changed since I was last there.

"What a charming young woman," Jewle said quietly.

I said I'd always found her so. I told him about her marriage and what I knew about Frank Sievers, but before I could finish she'd appeared again.

"You can see him now," she said. "The doctor might be coming in any time soon, if you'd like to see him too."

Jewle and I went in. Bernard was propped up on the pillows, a bandage round his head. There was quite a wad of sticking-plaster at the corner of his mouth. I smiled down at him.

"Well, young fellow, this is a nice state of affairs. How're you feeling?"

"Not too bad," he said, and made rather a poor hand of a grin. "It's these damn ribs, principally. You have to be careful how you move."

"This is Superintendent Jewle," I said. "He just came along for the ride."

"I know. Greta told me. Do sit down."

We sat down. Greta must have brought in an extra chair.

"Feel like telling me all about it?" Jewle said.

He said there wasn't a lot to tell. It had all happened so suddenly. What he'd intended the previous evening was to see a film, so he'd had an early meal at a little restaurant he knew near Oxford Circus. He got home at about seven, and as soon as he let himself in and switched on the light he heard a noise in the bedroom. He opened the bedroom door and switched on the light and there was the man.

"What was he like?"

"Shortish and thick-set. He had on a dirty-looking rain-coat and was wearing gloves. I think he was about fifty."

"You'd recognise him again?"

"Oh yes," he said. "I'd recognise him anywhere. I said to him 'Who the devil are you?' and 'What're you doing here?' Something like that. Then he began coming towards me shouting 'Get out of my bloody way', but I didn't. Then he hollered again and kept coming. Next thing I knew he'd caught me here on the side of the mouth. I started to yell for help and I don't really know what happened. The doctor says I was kicked on the head and the ribs."

"A nasty experience," Jewle said. "Were those blinds drawn, by the way?"

"No, they weren't."

"Then the man might have been visible from the far side of the road. You know that someone heard the rumpus and dialled 999?"

"Yes," he said. "The police said something about it last night."

"Whoever it was didn't come up here?"

"Don't know," he said. "If he did, I didn't see him. I'd passed out."

"Of course." Jewle smiled down at him. "You either did a brave thing or a damn silly one. Depends which way you look at it. Next time you meet a tough customer like that, open the street door for him and show him out. And just one other thing. Soon as you're well enough we'd like you to come along to Scotland Yard and look at some pictures. You might be able to spot your man."

There was a tap at the door. Greta looked in.

"The doctor's here."

We went out. The youngish doctor gave us a nod as he went through. He closed the door behind him.

"Would you like some coffee? I was just about to make some for myself and Bernard?"

"That's very nice of you," Jewle said. "Mrs. Sievers, isn't it?"

"Yes," she said. "I used to be Greta Morren. Bernard's sister. Or did Mr. Travers tell you that?"

She disappeared through the door which I'd thought led to her bedroom. Through the door of Bernard's room we could just hear the voices.

"Another cup won't harm us," Jewle told me. "Might as well hear all we can. You gathered anything so far?"

I shrugged my shoulders. "Only, as you said, that he was a bit of a fool to tangle with a chap like that."

A minute or two and the bedroom door opened. The doctor came out. He shifted his bag to his left hand and held the right hand out to Jewle.

"You're from Scotland Yard?"

"That's right," Jewle said. "The name's Jewle. This is a friend of Bernard's—Mr. Travers."

I got a smile and a nod. Greta must have heard us. We didn't even hear her till she was in.

"How was he, Doctor?"

"Doing well," he said. "A couple of days and he might get up for a bit. It might be a fortnight before he stops feeling the ribs."

"What about food?"

He laughed. "Just fill him up. At his age I could eat a horse. Nothing that takes too much chewing. The jaw's still a bit sore."

She smiled. "You've been very good. I'm just making some coffee. Will you stay for a cup?"

"Too busy," he said. "Thank you all the same."

"Then perhaps you'll excuse me."

She went off to the kitchen again. Jewle gave a little cough. "Tell me, Doctor. What sort of shape was he in when you saw him last night?"

"Not too good. It was a most vicious attack. If that kick on the head, for instance, had been a bit more to the right he might have been killed. The sooner you people lay your hands on the burglar the better." He held out his hand. "Sorry I have to be going. If you want anything from me you've only to ring. The name's Harbison. G. L. Harbison. You'll find me in the directory."

Jewle closed the door after him. Greta came in with the coffee tray, this time through Bernard's room. Somehow I still hadn't got the layout of that apartment.

I moved the low table near to the settee and the three of us sat down. Greta poured the coffee. It tasted good.

"Must have been an awful shock to you, Mrs. Sievers," Jewle said. "I mean being suddenly called here last night."

She smiled. "The police were very good, really. They just played it down a bit. Said he'd had a slight accident and might have to be in bed for a few days. That's why I brought a case with me."

"What did Frank, your husband, think of it?" I said.

"He's away for at least a week. His people have opened a branch in Paris and he's keeping an eye on it."

"And your small daughter? What's her name, by the way?"

She smiled.

"Susan Greta. Father wanted the Greta. I chose the Susan. She's a darling. You must come and see her some time."

"I'd love to. She has a nannie of course. I mean, otherwise you couldn't be here."

"A nannie, and a housekeeper." She laughed, and for a moment she looked just as she'd been three years ago. "We Sieverses do ourselves pretty well."

"And why not? Didn't Bernard tell me you were living at Northwood?"

"Overlooking the golf-course," she said. "It's quiet but we like it enormously."

"You mean you don't miss all the excitement of the boutique?"

"Perhaps a little bit," she said. "Helen was really a very lovely person. Maybe one day. After we've finished raising a family."

There'd been no old-fashioned blush.

"What about you, Superintendent?" She'd realised that Jewle was being left out of things. "Have you any children?"

"Two," he said. "Grown-up, I'm afraid. As a matter of fact. I'm a grandfather."

He began getting to his feet. "That was a perfectly delicious cup of coffee. We're both very grateful. And now we must hurry away. If I'm ever out Northwood way, I'd very much like to look you up."

"Do," she said. "Both of you. We'd love to see you. All three of us."

"Let's cross the road," Jewle said. "I'd like to have a look at that window."

Those premises consisted only of the shop and the apartment above it, but the shop was particularly high-ceilinged, so that the whole property had nothing by any means squat about it. The window of Bernard's room seemed surprisingly high up as we looked at it from the far pavement.

"Suppose it's night and the light's on up there," Jewle said. "How much would you see?"

"Not much," I said. "Probably only the head and shoulders of anyone who was looking through the window."

We crossed the street again and walked on to the car. It was almost cosy there after the bitter wind outside.

"About that window," Jewle said. "I was thinking in terms of the man who dialled 999. He couldn't have seen anything. According to Morren, there wasn't any noise till the burglar began approaching him, which would have taken him completely out of view from the road. So what the caller was alarmed by was the noise."

I began to see what he was driving at. "You think even the noise would hardly have been heard?"

Jewle smiled. "I ask you. Even at night there's traffic along here. There're people. It isn't as if it's all that quiet, and yet one special man hears from up in that apartment what was called a disturbance. Is it feasible?"

"But there *was* a disturbance."

"I know," he said patiently. "For one thing, Morren was yelling for help. My point is that, coming from a closed room all that high up, it wouldn't have been heard. But it *was* heard and therefore it must have been from somewhere else. And that must have been the landing outside the flat door."

"Just a minute," I said. "Let me think this out. It was what the caller *saw* that made him suspicious, so he followed the man up to the landing and heard the noise there." I shook my head. "The burglar must have been behaving in a damn silly way for him to have done that."

"I know," Jewle said. "The only explanation, as I see it, is this. The caller and the burglar were confederates. The caller was the look-out man. When he saw Morren unexpectedly enter the passage, he went up the stairs after him and listened at the door. When the rumpus started he got the wind up. He might have thought his burglar pal was going too far. Or the burglar might have realised he'd gone too far with Morren and told him to ring the police and then skip it. Which was what the caller did. Wouldn't give a name and wasn't about when the police arrived."

"Could have been," I said. "But two on the job must have meant something more important than just a chance breaking-in. What were they after?"

"Ah!" he said. "Now we're coming to it. Put yourself in my place this morning. I hear the name Morren. I look at the report myself. A burglary at Karl Morren's son's flat. What comes into my mind?"

"Diamonds."

"Exactly. I didn't wait for it to make any more sense. I just rang you. That's why I told you I might have brought you here on a fool's errand."

That much was clear. Quite a lot wasn't.

"Suppose you were right," I said. "That presupposes two things: that Bernard Morren either had the diamonds or they were hidden in the flat, and that the burglar was Wayner's accomplice when the diamonds were stolen."

"That's what came into my mind," Jewle said. "That was why I rang you. Also I remembered that Wayner had been released only that morning and he'd be looking for his accomplice. And the diamonds. What I now think is that it was Wayner himself who was acting as look-out man last night and Wayner who dialled 999."

I think the rather stupid question I asked was to make a little time to think it all out. "What about the door lock?"

"You saw it," Jewle said. "A Yale lock. No trouble at all to anyone who's learned the knack."

"You know what I'm beginning to think?" I said. "What we've got is only a part of the truth. It's like something that'd be right if only you could arrange the pieces in a different way. Or else there's something else missing. What worries me is that I'd bet my last dollar that Bernard Morren never let himself be mixed up in anything crooked. In any case he couldn't have had anything to do with the actual theft. He and his sister must have left the flat at about six that night so as to get to their uncle's hotel by half-past. And why, once the diamonds were taken, an accomplice should have gone to the flat and hidden the diamonds there sounds to me like sheer lunacy."

"I know," he said. "There's the hell of a lot wrong but there's also the hell of a lot right. Nobody's going to convince me that last night's job was just what it seems on the face of it."

He settled himself in the driver's seat.

"You don't think I did wrong to call you?"

"No," I said. "You were absolutely right. Don't ask me why. All I know is that you were."

He wanted to know where he could drop me. I didn't want to take him out of his way, so I got out at the Yard and took a Liverpool Street bus.

I was actually talking over the morning's happenings with Norris when Hallows rang.

"Think we've struck oil," he said. "A middle-class hotel called the Sandford. In Sandford Street. Turn left about a couple of hundred yards south of Baker Street, going toward Oxford Circus. A man answering roughly to Wayner's description booked in at the right time with the right number of cases."

I said I'd be along straightaway.

It was well after midday when I got out at Baker Street. There was no trouble in finding Sanford Street. The hotel itself was about another hundred yards along, on the corner with Tredgold Street. That meant there'd be two entrances. I looked across from the main entrance for a point of observation, and then I saw Hallows emerging from what turned out to be a small restaurant: one of those places that mushroom up and mushroom out. French, he said, would be reporting back at six to take over the evening shift.

He said the food at the restaurant was primitive but edible. We played for safety with cold ham, chips and coffee.

"What I thought of doing after I'd seen you was to book a room at the hotel," he said. "Wayner's on the second floor in Number 65. I ought to be able to get something near. I tipped the hall porter. He hasn't seen anything of Wayner since he booked in. Keep him happy and he'll lend a hand."

I told him about my morning with Jewle. He, too, thought there was something in it, though just what he didn't know.

"Wayner had a free hand last night," he said. "He might have gone anywhere. My man's the day porter this week, so he wouldn't know."

I asked about the twin entrances. He'd admitted that'd make things a bit tricky. The self-operated lift was at the far end of the main hall, with the Tredgold Street entrance immediately to the left as you emerged. Not that it would matter. If Wayner's room was under observation he'd be followed down. Which way he chose to leave the hotel wouldn't matter.

That was how we left things. I walked through to Oxford Circus and took the Underground to the Bank. Five stations in a matter of about ten minutes. That made it handy to get from Broad Street back to Sanford Street again. I'd been back about an hour when Hallows reported he'd been lucky about a room. He had 72, only three doors along a short corridor. He wanted me to ring French and put him in the picture.

I ought to have been reasonably pleased, but I wasn't. What worried me was not what might happen but what might have happened already while Wayner had been free to go where he wished. He'd arrived circuitously at an hotel which he'd had in mind from the very first. He'd known just what he was going to do and maybe he'd done it. Whether or not that affair at Bernard Morren's flat was part of the plan, I had no means of knowing. I still couldn't make sense of it in any case.

I stayed on at the agency that night till Hallows rang again. He said he was ringing from his hotel room and

French had just come on duty. Wayner's room seemed empty at the moment.

I went home and almost at once Hallows rang me again.

"Thought I'd have a word with the night porter before I left. Wayner's registered under the name Raymond, by the way, and the hall porter saw him come in last night about eight o'clock. Another man was just behind him and they took the lift almost together. A tallish, burly man. They didn't seem to know each other."

11. THE DURFORD MYSTERY

WHEN I reached the agency the next morning, and still a bit earlier than my usual time, I found French waiting for me. He said Hallows had taken over at seven that morning as arranged and had wanted him, French, to make a personal report to me about what had happened the previous night. I ought to have known it wasn't just routine.

"And what did happen?" I said.

"We've lost Wayner," he said. "What I mean is, I lost him. He slipped me last night, but all his things are still there. He'll almost certainly be back."

At about half-past seven the previous night Wayner had left his room and gone down to the hotel restaurant for a meal. He'd taken his time over it and it wasn't till ten minutes to eight that he went up to his room again. When he came out he had on a dark overcoat, thick gloves but no hat. He waited in the entrance hall for a minute or two and once or twice looked up at the clock. At eight o'clock he went out to Tredgold Street. He stood indecisively on the pavement as if undecided which way to go. There was a fair amount of traffic both ways, which was why French hadn't paid any particular attention to a private car that had drawn in a few yards beyond the hotel in the Baker Street direction.

When Wayner moved off towards Baker Street, French still had no reason to associate him with the car. In fact Wayner was in it and had moved off into the traffic stream before French could make a move. Another car masked the number but it was definitely a Ford Anglia.

"Could have happened to anyone," I said. "And he didn't come back last night?"

"He wasn't back when I left," he said. "We fixed it with the chambermaid to have a look in his room, and his bed hadn't been slept in and all his things were there."

I told him to get back home. If anything happened before he was due to report in the evening, he'd be rung. But I didn't like it. I didn't like it at all. Nothing had gone right for us since Wayner had left The Carlo almost two days before, and what had now happened looked like the finishing stroke. What Hallows would think I didn't know, but to me it looked like folly to go on with the case at all. Wayner could by now have made any contact he liked.

Hallows rang in the middle of the morning. Yes, I said, French had reported.

"Our friend still isn't back," he said. "Anything you can suggest?"

There was nothing except that we keep up the observation for, say, another twenty-four hours.

"I think he may possibly have spent the night with a lady friend," he said. "She might have been driving the car that picked him up. The interesting thing'll be what he does when he turns up. My guess is that he'll check out. If he does, we'll know he has money in his pocket. Not much we can do after that."

His pessimism was blatant optimism compared with what I was thinking. Then, not more than five minutes later, Bertha told me Jewle wanted a word.

"You remember a private enquiry agent named Kenneth Durford?" he said. "You had an idea he might have been mixed up with a certain lady in that Corby Street job."

"You're going a long way back," I said. "That was just after Wayner went to jail."

"Well, he's suddenly cropped up again," he said. "Are you busy? If not, I'll pick you up in about twenty minutes."

Broad Street wasn't far out of his way if we went by Islington and Highbury. He had a driver and so we could talk. What he wanted me to do was to tell him everything that had transpired between Durford and me when I'd seen him in his Wood Green office. It took some remembering, but I think I gave him the gist of it.

He didn't comment. He gave me some news instead.

"I ought to have told you what all this is about. It appears that Durford's son-in-law reported to the local police that his father-in-law was missing! I didn't tell you at the time—no special need to—that I saw the local police myself three or so years ago and had a confidential word about Durford. If anything had come of it, I'd have told you, but it didn't. But that's why I was rung this morning immediately after the son-in-law reported Durford was missing. I suppose you can throw no light on it?"

I told him I hadn't the least idea. I'd had no contact with Durford. I hadn't even thought of him since I'd seen him that day in his office. We'd had an understanding, as I'd said, that he'd pass on to the agency, and we'd pay him for, anything he might discover about the missing diamonds. Nothing had been heard from him.

"Then we'd better leave it till we hear what it's all about," Jewle said. "Probably nothing whatever to do with that old case. If it turns out to be a wasted morning I'll stand you a lunch."

The car drew in opposite the tobacconist's shop. Harold Anstell, the son-in-law, wasn't there. His wife said he was in the office upstairs. All she knew was that the previous night her father should have returned Harold's car, and he hadn't. And he hadn't turned up that morning either. She'd made her husband report it to the police in case there'd been an accident.

We went up the passage stairs to the office. Anstell was waiting for us. He was an intelligent, well-spoken man in the early thirties. When Jewle introduced himself and me I expected some sign of surprise that a big name at Scotland Yard should be occupying himself with what might turn out to be a car accident. Anstell wasn't surprised at all.

"He's been acting very queerly the last two or three days," he said. "The first I heard about it was from Len Howard. He owns a couple of taxis, one of which he drives himself. He's a great friend of mine, and when he came in the shop yesterday morning he told me confidentially what my father-in-law had been up to. He said he couldn't tell me everything but his taxi had been hired for the whole day previous."

"But your father-in-law was an enquiry agent," Jewle said. "Surely there were times when he had to hire a taxi, even for a whole day."

"If he did, then it wasn't Len's," he said. "If he's on a job that involves travelling he always borrows my car. Just as he did last night."

He told us about it. He and his wife lived just off Bound's Green Road, which was where he kept the car.

But perhaps you'd better get the dates in mind. That morning was a Saturday, so it was on a Thursday that Wayner had been released. On the Wednesday evening Durford had paid a visit, as he often did. The two grandchildren were in bed, and after seeing them he said he was going to be on an important job the next day and would he—Anstell—take any calls. Anstell apparently often did that: just a matter of moving a special switch to the shop. Durford wouldn't stay to supper but left not long after seven.

"The next thing was, he rang me at the shop from somewhere or other yesterday morning," Anstell went on. "He said would I go on taking calls. And could he borrow the car that night. If so, he'd pick it up at about seven o'clock. I said, of course he could have it. As a matter of fact I was there when he came for it and I got it out for him. I asked him when he'd be back and he said it might be late. Probably not before eleven, and I wasn't to wait up. And that's the last I saw of him. I looked in the garage this morning and the car wasn't back."

"Probably something happened to take him further afield," Jewle said.

"Then why didn't he ring me? He could have. He hasn't even rung this morning."

"I know." Jewle said. "It's one of the things that've been worrying you. What was the number of the car?"

"GK-710," he said. "A Ford Anglia. Pale yellow. 1962."

I'd given Jewle a surreptitious prod, which was why he'd suspended temporarily any further talk with Anstell, except to get the address of Len Howard. Anstell had pointed out that it was a Saturday. Len himself always stopped work at noon on a Saturday. As a football fan, he liked to watch either the Arsenal or Spurs.

We'd found Len Howard's place first. By the side of the house was a largish yard with quite a big garage. We went past it a little way and then I began putting Jewle in the picture: how Wayner had slipped us on the Thursday: hadn't been located till the Friday morning, and finally about a Ford Anglia that had picked him up in Tredgold Street at eight o'clock that night. He asked me to go over it in detail again.

"So Wayner isn't back either," he said. "That ought to mean he and Durford are still together somewhere."

"Then why hasn't Durford rung? He must know that Anstell and his wife would be anxious."

"You'd think so," he said. "Let's see if we can find Howard."

Howard was in. His wife said he was changing his clothes upstairs. Could she take a message? Jewle said he'd be obliged if he could wait, so she showed us into a little sitting-room and lighted the gas fire.

Howard joined us in about five minutes. He was about Anstell's age; pleasant-faced and alert-looking. The look was much more serious as soon as Jewle had introduced himself.

"Something's wrong, sir?"

"Not necessarily," Jewle said. "Only that Kenneth Durford didn't come home last night after borrowing his son-in-law's car. Don't get alarmed. You'd nothing to do with it. All I want from you is an exact account of what you and Durford did together last Thursday. I know, by the way, that it wasn't anything illegal, but just tell us all about it. Start from the beginning and take your time."

It didn't come out all in one piece, but this is what it amounted to. On the previous Wednesday, Durford had seen him and put up a proposition. He wanted to hire Howard and his taxi for the following day, beginning at about nine the next morning. He put all his cards on the table. Howard heard for the first time about Wayner and the diamonds.

"He said he'd found out that Wayner was being released at ten the next morning, so he wanted us to follow him. It sounded all right to me, so I agreed. I picked Ken up at his place at nine and we went straight to the prison and waited. Ken pointed him out when he came out and I followed him to Finsbury Park, where he went into a big club of some sort called The Carlo. It was a big Humber that'd picked him up, but when he left it was in a taxi. We saw it come up and we followed it when it left. When Ken saw it was turning into Charing Cross station he told me to get in behind, and as soon as this Wayner got out I was to move my cab on and make out something was wrong: an excuse, see, for staying on. Then a porter took this Wayner's luggage and Ken followed. I moved on a bit and started looking for what was wrong with my cab. A couple of minutes and this Wayner came out through the hotel door carrying a bag. He waited a minute or so for another taxi and got a porter to fetch his luggage again. Soon as it came he took a taxi and we followed him.

"When he got out at Baker Street Station, Ken told me to find somewhere to park, which I did. When I got back, Ken wasn't there, so I waited. When he turned up he said it was all right. No need for me to wait. 'He's putting up at an hotel,' he said, 'so you might as well go home. I'll settle up with you tomorrow.'"

"Which he did?"

"Yes, sir. He paid me five quid."

"And that was all you heard about this day of yours? He didn't tell you anything else later?"

"Not a thing, sir. I was supposed to keep my mouth shut in any case. I wasn't supposed to know anything about this Wayner."

"Right," Jewle said. "Thank you for your co-oper-ation. Oh, and just one thing. Durford got you to help him follow this man Wayner. Didn't he give any specific reason? What I'm getting at is this. Wayner was being released. He'd served his sentence and was free. So why follow him?"

"Don't know, sir. He told me about this Wayner getting four years for taking some diamonds—"

Something was coming back.

"That's it," he said. "I remember now. He said the job was being done for some interested parties. They wanted to know where this Wayner went to."

"He mentioned nothing about a reward for the diamonds if they were recovered?"

"No, sir; not a word."

Jewle held out his hand. "That's all, Mr. Howard. You've been most helpful. Just one other thing. If Mr. Durford should happen to ring you, let the local police know."

He gave me a questioning look, but I had nothing to ask. A minute or two later Jewle was asking his driver to stop short of the main road.

"I may have to hang about here quite a time," he told me. "Are you prepared to wait or would you rather get back to town?"

I said I'd plenty to do. For one thing, I wanted to establish a closer connection between Durford and Wayner, and I ought to be able to do it at the hotel.

"Just one thing I'd like to work out," he said. "This man Durford once did a job for Morren's wife."

"When she *was* his wife," I said. "They're divorced. Have been for a couple of years."

He said it didn't make any difference. Durford did a job for her and Durford had told Howard that Wayner was to be followed because certain parties were interested. Was there any truth in it? Was Durford employed by the former Beryl Morren? And if so, why?

"A bit too much to answer at a minute's notice," I said. "If it ever becomes necessary, you could ask her. No use my trying to do it."

He said he'd think it over. I asked to be dropped near the Tube station. I'd be going straight to Baker Street and the Sanford Hotel and from there back to the agency if he wanted to get in touch.

As soon as my train moved off I began working on that problem Jewle had put: whether or not Durford had been working for Beryl Lambourn. Even when the time came to change trains I hadn't found an answer. On the whole,

I was inclined to think Durford was working as a free-lance. He'd taken care, for instance, not to mention that matter of a reward: still probably valid even after nearly three years. I remembered, too, that on that morning when I'd followed Durford from the Old Bailey to Wood Green what we'd principally talked about had been that reward. I'd offered to buy anything he discovered about the Corby Street job, but had heard nothing from him, so maybe he'd gone on working quietly on his own. By the time Wayner was due for release he'd worked out a course of action.

Hallows was sitting in the main hall of the hotel reading a newspaper. He looked over the top as I came in. He told me nothing whatever had happened. I was feeling a bit hungry, so we talked over lunch. There were a lot of loose ends to tie up before he could get the full import of everything I'd learned that morning.

"So it was Durford's taxi I saw that morning," he said. "It looked like a trail job at the time. A pretty smart trick, getting the taxi-owner to help. No wonder I lost Wayner."

That was water under the bridge. What we had to find out was when Durford had first made direct contact with Wayner.

"Far as I remember," I said, "it was learned from the night porter that Wayner was out somewhere that first evening here, and when he came in again at about eight o'clock another man came in practically on his heels. I think you should have another word with that porter and get him to give a description of the man."

There was only the sweet course to come, so he said he'd do it at once. The night porter was on the telephone and he had his number. He was away for about ten minutes, and from the brisk way he came back I guessed he had something.

"The man was Durford," he said. "No doubt about it. He let Wayner go up alone in the lift and then went up himself."

So Durford had been on Wayner's heels from the time Wayner had booked in. He could have approached him as soon as he was settled in his room, but he didn't. He'd waited. Waited for what? To see if Wayner would make contact with some third party?

Whether Wayner had or hadn't, something must have happened to make Durford decide to approach Wayner direct. The hall porter hadn't seen Durford come down, so he might have been talking to Wayner in his room. He couldn't very well have taken the risk of hanging about in the corridor and keeping Wayner under observation: also that was a job he could just as well have done downstairs.

"So on Thursday night something was decided between Durford and Wayner," I said. "Something was going to be done, but it was too late to do it that night. Also there wasn't a car available. But there could be one the following night. Watches were synchronised, so to speak, and Durford was to pick Wayner up last night at eight o'clock, which he did."

That was merely bolting the stable door. What we had no means of discovering was where the horses had gone. Hallows was more optimistic about it than I. Sooner or later Durford would turn up. Police questioning might produce the right answers. What I didn't say was that Durford would have every right to keep his mouth shut.

Even if he decided to talk, it would most likely be to tell a tale previously decided on.

"If Durford turns up, then the police won't have any further interest," was what I said. "All his son-in-law did was report him and the car missing."

I had to get back to the agency in case Jewle might want to contact me. Hallows would be staying on in case Wayner came back. If he did, then we'd have to find out if Durford had come back too. If he hadn't, then the police would have every right to do some questioning.

Jewle rang me just after four o'clock. He sounded very abrupt.

"Some news about Durford. I'll pick you up as soon as I can get to Broad Street. That all right?"

I said it was. He rang off at once. He picked me up twenty minutes later. The same driver; the same car.

"You're not going to like it about Durford." he said, "I might as well tell you straight out. He's dead."

It hit me clean in the wind.

"Found lying by the side of the road last night." he said. "They got him to hospital, but he died on the way."

"He talked?"

"Never recovered consciousness. It was a bitterly cold night, and he'd probably been lying there for over an hour. In a quiet little side road north of New Barnet."

"And Wayner?"

"No sign of him. Or the car."

For a minute or two I didn't feel like talking. Just what I felt I didn't know, but there's a shattering finality about death. I hadn't liked Durford and I hadn't disliked him. Perhaps I was thinking about his daughter.

"You think it may be murder?"

"Won't know till I've seen the full reports," he said. "Enough, though, to get the call out for Wayner and the car."

"He might be anywhere. Even abroad."

"Depends on where we find the car," he said. "Wherever he was making for, he's had a twenty-hour start."

At Palmers Green we turned left for Southgate and Chase Side, then left again through Barnet and on to New Barnet. The car slowed till it turned into a side road; quickened again for a minute or two and slowed again. A couple of men were standing on the grass verge and another car was drawn up just beyond them. We drew in a few yards short.

It was an inspector and his sergeant from the local C.I.D. "This is where he was found, sir," the inspector said. He flashed his torch. "You can see a little blood on the grass."

"What about the people who found him?"

Their statement had been taken. A man and his wife who lived at New Barnet had been returning at about ten o'clock from visiting friends at Cockfosters when they saw the man lying on the verge. He was obviously badly hurt, so the wife drove on to the nearest telephone. The man was still breathing when the police and the ambulance arrived. The man died in the ambulance on the way to the hospital.

"No means of identification on him?"

"Nothing at all, sir. Nothing in his pockets but a handkerchief and some loose change. Not even a wallet. No laundry marks on the handkerchief."

What had happened had been hard to decide. The stomach had had no alcoholic content, so he wasn't a drunk who had fallen in the path of an oncoming car. He just might have been attacked by some casual thief; but what with taking statements and getting reports, a general description hadn't been circulated till latish the next morning.

"Right," Jewle said. "Let's go and have a look at him."

We had to move on before we could reverse. We followed the other car to the hospital. I'm foolishly squeamish about identifications, but it was I who had to have a look when the sheet was drawn back.

"Durford," I said. "No doubt about it."

Jewle had a good look at the wound. It was more like a deepish indentation.

"What do you make of it?" he said.

I could make nothing.

"And you, Inspector?"

"Might have been done with the butt of a heavy revolver. Say a Mark Six Webley."

"Yes," Jewle said. "You're probably right."

We moved on to the station. Jewle began reading the reports and passed them on to me. The wound was described by the doctor as a very heavy blow. The rest were merely confirmations of what we'd already been told.

We were asked if we'd like some tea. Jewle said we wouldn't be staying. He'd get into touch with the inspector later that evening; meanwhile he'd better ring the dead man's son-in-law. After that we went out to the car. We didn't move off at once. He asked me what I made of it all.

I said it seemed a bit too obvious. Wayner had been stringing Durford along. He'd seen him as a menace to something and he'd planned what had to be done. Durford had been told some cock-and-bull story—

That was where Jewle interrupted me. "Was it cock-and-bull? Where was the car heading for?"

"Cockfosters," I said. "It was the only logical place it could go."

"Right," Jewle said. "And Morren, the one who lost the diamonds, lives there. Wayner could have twisted it round so that Durford would think they were going to see Morren." There was something a bit wrong about that, but I didn't say so. That side road where Durford had been found wasn't the direct route to Cockfosters.

"Know what I think," Jewle was going on. "All Wayner really wanted was to get Durford to take some quiet road or other. What he was really after was the car. Get the number-plates changed and he'd be mobile. He could go anywhere."

"Except that his description will be circularised."

"It was done as soon as I heard about Durford," Jewle said. "The trouble is that Wayner might be anywhere by now. John o' Groats or Land's End. Even out of the country."

"So what now?"

"Two short visits," Jewle said. "Better try Karl Morren first."

12. DEAD END

IT TOOK longer to find Morren's house than it did to get to Cockfosters. It was three years since I'd been there, and we'd come in from a different direction, and finally we had to go to the Tube station before I managed to get the right road.

We left the car at the kerbside outside the house. It was dark in the servants' quarters above the garage, but a light was showing through the fanlight window of the porch door. The door was opened by the same woman who'd admitted me three years before. She seemed vaguely to recognise me too.

Jewle asked if Mr. Morren was in. He was. Jewle gave his name and we were asked to wait. Another minute and she was showing us into the lounge. The television was on and Morren turned it off as we came in. He looked very much older than when I'd last seen him. Then he'd merely been spare: now he was thin. The hair round the temples was quite white.

"You remember me?" Jewle said.

"Indeed, yes," Morren said. "You enquired into that diamond burglary three years ago."

"Perhaps you remember me too," I said. "Travers. I was here about that theft from your safe."

"Of course," he said. "Won't you sit down? Nothing serious this time, I hope."

"We're not staying," Jewle said. "Just want to ask you one question. You naturally remember Wayner? The man convicted of the robbery? It may seem a silly question, but did he by any chance happen to call on you last night?"

"On me!" he said. "You must be joking. Why on earth should he call on me?"

"Frankly, I don't know. Just the vague connection. You were robbed of the diamonds and he was the one who took them. Also we know he was heading this way last night in a car."

"I don't care which way he was heading." Morren was getting the least bit annoyed. "I wasn't even aware the man had been released."

"I'm sorry." Jewle said. "You know how things are. I have to ask questions. This man Wayner stole a car last night at about nine o'clock only a mile or two from here, and the one possible connection we could find was yourself. We thought he might conceivably have come here and had the nerve to sell you the diamonds back."

"That was a poor opinion of me." Morren told him. "It's assuming, if any such thing happened, I'd have kept it to myself. Not rung the police."

"I know, sir. The way I put it, it sounds bad. No offence was intended. Perhaps you weren't even here last night."

"I was. It was like any other night. I try to be considerate to my staff. Superintendent. That's why I have my evening meal as early as half-past six. That gives them the chance to have everything cleared away and washed up by eight, and then the rest of the evening's their own, so to speak. If I should happen to want one of them I've only to ring their flat. Last night I didn't see them after the meal. I watched television till just after ten o'clock; then I went to bed. Nobody called; nobody rang."

Jewle gave a disarming smile. "I'm sorry. Nothing I've said was intended to annoy you. Quite the contrary. We're grateful for your help. At least we now know where Wayner *wasn't* last night."

"That's all right," he said, still a bit grudgingly. "May I offer you both a drink? Or perhaps you'd like to speak to the staff?"

"That won't be necessary," Jewle said. "Your own word's more than enough. Thank you for the offer of a drink. Some other time, perhaps. We've got to be getting along."

Morren saw us to the door. He switched on a light that showed up the drive and saw us back in the car before he switched it off.

"A bit edgy, wasn't he?" Jewle said.

"I think I'd have been," I told him. "You asked him some highly suggestive questions. Also, he's had a very bad time this last year or so."

"His business?"

Jewle asked it a bit too quickly.

"No," I said. "His second marriage."

I told him about it.

"Naturally I never met her myself," I said, "but I do know the Morren children didn't think much of her. Bernard called her a bit cheap. I think that was the word he used. Where're we going now?"

He had looked to me as if we were making for Hendon.

"West Hampstead," he said. "Beryl What's-her-name is going to tell us what she knew about Durford."

"The name's Lambourn," I told him. "She married an Arthur Lambourn who runs a gaming club at Knightsbridge. You've heard of him? Bernard Morren called him a very decent sort of chap."

We made for the police station. I stayed put. When Jewle came back he knew where to find Beryl Lambourn—at a newish block of flats called Norland House.

It was an expensive-looking block: wide entrance, parking space in front, nicely manicured rosebuds—everything, indeed, one would hope to get for, say, nine hundred a year. Inside, things were even more handsome. Jewle had a word with a very handsome receptionist at the long, mahogany desk, and then we walked up the handsomely carpeted steps and along a corridor to Flat 4. It was Beryl who opened the door.

She looked younger and definitely better-humoured than when I'd seen her last. Marriage with Lambourn must have been very much of a tonic, or was it release from Karl Morren?

Jewle introduced himself. Me she remembered. That's what often makes things difficult. Nobody forgets me. I can't switch myself around. A lean six-feet and more and the huge horn-rims see to that.

She showed us in. It wasn't a furnished flat. Too many period pieces for that. The huge Chinese carpet would have been a bargain at four hundred pounds. The two groups on the mantelshelf looked like pre-Marcolini Dresden.

"What a charming room!" I said.

"My husband comes of a very old family," she told me. "These are his things, of course. Won't you both sit down and tell me what all this is about?"

We took the same settee by the electric fire. She settled herself in a chair opposite.

"We rather hoped you could tell *us*," Jewle said.

She gave him a quick look. "I don't understand you. You mean something to do with my former husband?"

"No," Jewle said. "But last night a man was murdered not far from Cockfosters. We think you know him. His name was Kenneth Durford."

As far as I could see, she didn't move a muscle. The steady look was still trained on Jewle.

"Durford?" She shook her head. "I'm afraid the name conveys nothing to me. Why did you think I knew him?"

"I'll tell you. Three years ago last March you employed him to do a job for you. He was a private enquiry agent."

Deny or confess? She made the quick decision. She smiled. "Oh, *that* Durford! I'm afraid I'd forgotten all about him."

"And now you've remembered." There was just a touch of irony. "Perhaps you also remember exactly why you employed him."

"But of course. It was to follow my husband. My then husband—Karl Morren."

"Would you give a little more detail?"

"Why not?" she said. "Karl used to be away far too much on what he called valuations, and I began to be suspicious. I asked a friend about a private detective and she found me this man Durford, and he found out my suspicions were correct. He'd been keeping a woman. I hope I don't shock you."

Jewle smiled. "We're pretty case-hardened. But please go on."

"Well, it was the same woman whom he married after I divorced him."

"Pardon me," I said, "but wasn't it the other way about? Didn't he divorce you?"

She laughed. "Oh that! That was part of the bargain. I was to wait till my daughter got married and he was to pay my debts. I'm afraid I'd been a little bit extravagant."

"And you also had another husband in view?"

You could see she was thinking of being indignant, then she changed her mind. "I knew my present husband, if that's what you mean."

"Thank you," Jewle said. "But to get back to Durford. When did you next employ him?"

She stared. "Employ him? Are you mad? Why on earth should I employ him?"

"You didn't?"

She snorted indignantly. "Of course I didn't. I never set eyes on him again."

"You'd be prepared to swear to that?"

"Why not? Don't you believe me?"

Jewle got to his feet. "I believe you. But may I ask a last question. You haven't any idea who could have wanted to kill Durford?"

"Of course not. How could I?"

There was a final smile: a malicious one.

"Of course there was Karl. But then, poor dear, he never knew about Durford. He never could understand how I got hold of all those facts."

She showed us out. We went back along the handsome carpeting and across the tessellated floor of the hall and through the wide swing doors to the car.

"What a woman!" Jewle said. "If you ask me, it was a lucky day for Morren when she used Durford."

He told the driver to wait.

"I'm going back to the Yard. What about you?"

I said I'd take a train from West Hampstead and walk the few yards from Leicester Square. He told the driver to drop me.

"If that woman was telling the truth," he said, "it finally squashes that theory of yours—the one about collusion with Durford over the diamond robbery."

I had to agree.

"But it could be a reason why Durford was at the trial," I said. "Durford knew Morren, and the trial was about Morren's diamonds. That could have interested him, especially with the reward in his mind."

"Maybe," Jewle said. "The trouble is it doesn't help a lot. All it does is eliminate."

The car drew in at the station. I said I'd be getting in touch with Hallows. If anything happened in the course of the next few hours I'd let him know.

"No," he said. "You call your people off. We're taking over from now on."

From the station I rang French. To save time, he was to ring Hallows; then go home. I'd see them both in the morning. I rang Bernice to say I'd been detained but should be home in half an hour.

It had been a pretty long day and after the meal I was happy to sit and do nothing at all. Television didn't appeal, so I just sat. Bernice was reading a book and knitting at the same time. For her that's no feat at all. She often knits and reads while watching television. In any case, I just happened to notice something.

"Have I seen that blouse before?"

She laughed. "I wondered if you'd notice it. You like it?"

I did. Bernice is a brunette and the black and dark red went well with her hair.

"I bought it at that Helen Cambon place," she said. "I hadn't been there for such a long time."

I said I'd heard they were still in operation.

"They're doing very well," she said. "But a very strange thing happened: at least I thought it strange. I thought I'd like to speak to Greta Morren: that very nice young girl who'd waited on me before, and she said she wasn't with them any more. I asked what Greta was doing and Helen Cambon said she didn't know. I thought there was something curious going on—you know how it is: some scandal or other, so I asked if she had her address, and she didn't."

"You were right," I said. "I actually saw Greta very recently in connection with an enquiry we're making. She's married and living at Northwood. Has a small daughter too. She told me she hoped one day to go back to Helen Cambon's place. She spoke of her as a very nice person."

"She is," Bernice said. "She's most charming, and that was the curious thing. At one minute she was—well, just herself; and then, as soon as I began enquiring about Greta Morren, she just froze up."

I said there had to be some explanation. I'd keep my ear to the ground and maybe I'd find it. Greta herself had always struck me as a remarkably frank sort of person.

I went on with what the sight of that blouse had inter-rupted—thinking over the drama of the last few hours. A few more and the hue-and-cry would sound for Wayner. I thought about Durford. Sometimes an apt line will come unexpectedly into my mind, and then it was Hamlet's quick epitaph on Polonius—that rash, intruding fool. Durford had got well out of his depth when he'd tried to outsmart Wayner.

What I did know was that we were virtually out of things. There was nothing now that we could actually do unless Jewle should happen to request it. That's how Hallows saw things when I put it to him in the morning. In any case he had things to do, and so did French, and that left me with the option of carrying on alone. So I arranged to see John Hill. What had happened was too confidential to talk over on the phone.

He didn't take long to make up his mind. Murder and the recovery of stolen property were vastly different things. Wayner had disappeared, and perhaps the diamonds, or his share of the proceeds of their sale, had gone with him. Only when he was found could we perhaps ask the police to give us any information they might by then have unearthed about the diamonds.

So Othello's occupation was gone as far as the Morren diamonds case was concerned. Or so it appeared. But even when I'd agreed on that with John Hill, I was far from being as frank with myself. I was too deeply involved to close that case as abruptly as one closes a door. Curiosity and the urge to know the why and wherefore would see to that.

All that happened for a day or two was a sort of frustration. I learned more from the newspapers than from Jewle. In any case, he was probably feeling a bit frustrated too. Wayner had apparently disappeared entirely, and the people who'd soon be looking for him, if they weren't already, were Interpol.

"It's a certainty he'll never come back to the hotel," Jewle told me. "He wouldn't be such a fool."

I wasn't so sure. "I don't think he really intended to kill Durford. He hit too hard, that was all. He mayn't even know that Durford is dead—if he's where he can't get a newspaper."

Jewle gave a little snort. "What he intended and what he did don't have to be argued. It's what happened that matters. In any case I'm giving it just two more days and then I'm going through those things of his he left at the hotel. I expect you'd like to come along."

I did go along. It was just two days later, as he'd told me, and around ten in the morning. He could have impounded the lot and had them gone over at the Yard, but, like me, he wanted to be getting his teeth into something, and there was always the hope of unearthing some vital clue.

The two large suitcases had been only partially unpacked. Their contents were almost entirely clothes, and expensive clothes at that. Maybe they'd been a kind of stock-in-trade: they'd certainly been well looked after. Everything was good: shirts, ties, socks, evening suits, shoes with nicely fitting trees. There was no correspondence. The only thing apart from the clothes was a book. Quite a large book: *The World's Great Fights* by a Malcolm Enfield.

From Sandy, Christmas 1961

That was what was written inside. It looked as good as new. Even the jacket was untorn.

Jewle was trying to get hold of Harry Alders at The Carlo.

I was flicking over the pages of that book, and all at once I saw a piece of paper that had almost certainly been used as a bookmark. It was an old envelope, addressed to Sandy Scott at The Carlo. On the back of it some words were scribbled in pencil. I put it into my pocket.

Jewle was at last talking to Harry. I heard him mention an electric razor. He asked if Harry were sure about something and then he hung up.

"Nothing was left behind," he told me. "And, far as they know, he didn't have a spare razor."

The implications were obvious. Every single toilet article, as well as pyjamas and dressing-gown, was still in that room.

When Wayner had left it on the Friday night, he must definitely have intended to be back. It put quite a different complexion on things.

"He'd been stringing Durford along, as you said," was how Jewle was now seeing it. "What he really wanted was the car, so when he got to the right spot he held him up at the point of the gun and made him get out. Perhaps Durford got a bit obstreperous, so Wayner hit him. He didn't trouble to see what the effect of the blow had been but got in the car and drove off. I'd say he was going to drive back to here; collect his gear, pay his bill and get away. But he didn't. Get back here, I mean. So what happened?"

"He did look at Durford," I said. "Saw he was badly hurt, so decided to get away at once without coming back here."

We left it like that. All Wayner's possessions were put back in the cases and we took them down in the lift and out to Jewle's car. He had a word with the manager and that was about all. He dropped me at a Tube station and went back to the Yard.

I was taking off my overcoat—Bertha had asked about coffee—and was checking the pockets in case I was leaving anything in, when my fingers felt paper. It was that envelope. I hung up overcoat and hat and had a good look at it. On the back were a few doodling lines and then some lettering or words—

L,L, ST—GATE

That was all, except that just below was some more doodling.

I lighted my pipe, leaned back in the chair and tried to puzzle it out. A minute or two and I asked Bertha to get me Harry Alders at The Carlo.

"You may think this a silly question, Mr. Alders, but was there a telephone in Wayner's room at the gymnasium?"

"No," he said. "Just the one. In Sandy's office."

I thanked him and rang off. So far so good. A call had come for Wayner and he'd taken it in Sandy's room. There was something he wanted to make a note of, so he'd grabbed the handiest piece of paper, which had happened to be that old envelope.

In a minute or two I'd worked it out in greater detail. At first there'd been some talking and he'd doodled while he'd listened. Then had come the something he'd been waiting for. and after that more talk and more doodling.

But what that actual lettering meant was altogether beyond me. Try as I might I could make neither head nor tail of it, and then at last I realised it was probably a lot of ado about nothing at all. Why should some obscure lettering on the back of an envelope be of any real significance? The date mark on the envelope showed it to be almost four years old—the envelope, that is.

I'd probably have put it in the waste-paper basket if I hadn't noticed that it had been folded: for convenience, most likely, when putting it into a pocket. And if Wayner had put it in his pocket when he'd left Sandy's office, then he knew he'd have to refer to it for some reason or other. That seemed to give it a fresh importance, so I folded it in its original fold and put it inside the small notebook I always carry in my breast pocket.

I think I've said before that for years I've taken what you might call a topic to bed with me: something on which to focus my thoughts as soon as I feel the warmth of the bed: something that generally gets me in less than no time off to sleep. That night I thought about the envelope. For five minutes, perhaps, and then I was thinking of just nothing at all.

13. THE MIRACLE

IT HAPPENS, I imagine, to all of us. One goes to bed with a problem and wakes up to find it solved. At any rate that was what happened to me. When I woke up, I wasn't even thinking about that lettering on the back of an envelope, and then suddenly the answer, or part of it, was there.

I saw myself holding a pencil while someone at the other end of a telephone gave me instructions, and what I realised was that it was almost a certainty that what I was going to write down would be directions for getting somewhere. L might stand for Left. The ST held me up for a minute till I thought it might be STraight. The GATE might be short for a place with that ending—Margate, say, or Ramsgate. Or it might have something to do with the name of a house or road. In any case what I had as a solution was—*Turn left, left again, keep straight on and you'll come to—?*

As an answer to what now seemed a very minor problem, that was gratifying, but it didn't tell me anything about Wayner. He was the sort of oppression—the cloud on my mind—and when I'd cleared my desk at the agency I began thinking of him again. I wanted to be doing something: I needed a clue or even a hint to follow up without getting in the way of the police, and the only thing that came to mind was something that had a connection so vague as to be almost non-existent—the contradictory statements as to the present relationships between Greta Sievers and her former employer, Helen Cambon. I don't think that I'd have given it much thought, eager though I was for something to work at, if I hadn't thought of something else in the same context—that I might do worse than make a courtesy call on Bernard.

No sooner thought of than done. I took the Underground to Piccadilly Circus and walked on from there. I had a quick listen at the door of the apartment. I heard nothing and it struck me that he might have sufficiently recovered to have been able to go out. I was wrong. I waited only a few seconds after I'd rung, and he was opening the door. He seemed delighted to see me.

"Thought I'd see for myself how you were getting along," I said. "That was a very nasty experience of yours."

He said he was very much better. The ribs were mending: tightly strapped, in any case, so that it was fairly easy now to move.

"I'll be going back to the office at the beginning of the week. But do let me get you some coffee. I was just about to make some for myself."

He disappeared in the direction of the kitchen. The lounge was warm but I didn't take off my overcoat. It's easier to make extempore conversation when you're on the point of going than to make talk when it seems as if you're going to stay. That way you can often avoid answers.

Almost at once he came in with two steaming breakfast cups of coffee.

"One thing about it," I said. "You're nice and snug in here. When did your sister leave?"

"About a couple of days after you were here," he said. "Frank came back and there wasn't anything very urgent here."

"I can't help thinking what a pity it was she couldn't have carried on in business. So many married women do, even young mothers. She seemed so absolutely right for the job."

"Oh, she'd like it well enough," he said. "It's just a question of getting round Frank."

"She still keeps in contact?"

"Good lord, yes," he said. "Gets practically all her clothes there."

"And your burglar friend. You've heard nothing from the police?"

"They're still working on it," he said. "As a matter of fact, I've arranged to go to Scotland Yard early this afternoon to look at some of their photographs. They're sending a car for me."

"Maybe you'll be able to pick the man out. The police are pretty thorough people: far more so than they get credit for. Take this dreadful Wayner business. You've read about it?"

"Oh yes," he said. "Absolutely horrible. What's your own opinion? Do you think he's gone mad? I mean—well, robbery's one thing, but murder's another."

"Don't know," I said. "He was leading quite an athletic life before he went to jail. How'd you feel after being shut up for three years?"

The question was largely rhetorical. A minute or two later I was getting to my feet. I said I'd have to be going. I'd only dropped in to see how he was. I ought to have called before.

"Not at all, sir. It was awfully decent of you to come."

"Nothing you want? Books, for instance?" Then I had to laugh. "Rather a coals-to-Newcastle question."

"It's good of you, but I'm fixed up for everything." He held out his hand. "Most kind of you, though. I'm really grateful."

By the time I was back at Regent Street I was sure of the next port of call. Something, as Bernice had sensed, was very wrong. For Helen Cambon to have claimed that she had no idea of the present whereabouts of Greta Sievers was utter nonsense.

At Oxford Circus I managed to get a taxi. There seemed no reason why I shouldn't enquire about Greta myself. After all, I had a good excuse. She'd virtually invited me to see her small daughter whenever I was in the neighbourhood of Northwood, which I couldn't do if I didn't know the address. As far as asking Bernard—well, I'd just happened to forget.

I stopped the taxi at the south end of Gordon Street and walked on. In a couple of minutes I was at the shop— pardon me—boutique. It had quite a fair-sized frontage, and what I saw through the windows had definitely a touch of class. I braced my shoulders and walked in.

There was a delicious scent like old leather and Chanel No. 5. Plenty of racks but no counter: just a kind of desk. The woman who had been working there got up at once, and I guessed she was Helen Cambon. Everything about her said style: the dress she was wearing, the way she walked and even the formal smile that seemed something especially for myself.

"Good morning."

She waited. I gave a little bow.

"Good morning. I wonder if you could do me a favour. A friend of mine used to work here—Greta Morren. Could you let me have her present address?"

The smile was barely perceptible.

"I'm afraid not," she said. "If I knew it I'd be only too pleased. But I don't."

"Oh dear!" I shook my head. "Well, I just happened to be this way, so I thought I'd enquire. But could you do something else for me? Tell me the nearest way to a Tube station?"

She went to the door with me. What a charming woman she was: a brunette, rather like Bernice but cosily plump.

"It's the first to the right," she told me, "and then straight on. About two minutes' walk."

I thanked her again. As I moved off I was a long way from happy. Somehow I couldn't think that a woman like that could tell a deliberate lie. It seemed so utterly out of character. And yet, apparently, she had. Someone had certainly been lying: either Bernard Morren or Helen Cambon. And why should Bernard lie about his sister? All I could find by way of answer was that the quarrel, tiff—call it what you will—had arisen very recently. But even that was wrong. If the two women were no longer on speaking terms, surely Bernard should have mentioned it? I couldn't for the life of me see why not.

I came to the cross-roads. "First to the right," she'd said, so that was the turning I took. Then I almost stopped in my tracks. Something had come into my mind: something so startling that I had to get to somewhere quiet and think it over.

There was a coffee-shop a few yards on, so I went in. I no more wanted coffee than I wanted a wig, but it gave me a chance to sit and think.

Just that simple direction to take the right-hand turn and keep straight on had brought something to mind—that lettering on the back of an old envelope. The brain works in queer ways and somehow it had been associated with the Saturday night and how I hadn't been able at first to find Karl Morren's house. As I've said, I'd had to tell the driver to go to the Tube station and I'd take it from there.

And if I'd been directing anyone to Karl Morren's house, this is what I'd have said: "Take the first left, then left again and keep straight on. You'll know The Elms because the name's on the drive gate."

It was staggering. I could hardly believe it. But I didn't question it. I just knew it was right. Someone that distant day had been telling David Wayner how to get to The Elms, provided he came to Cockfosters by Tube.

But who? Definitely not the housekeeper or gardener. Karl Morren himself? If so, it might be the first step in explaining why Wayner had been making for Cockfosters on the Friday night. Which meant again that Morren had been lying to Jewle and myself.

Beryl Lambourn? Was she the one who had given him those directions? Last Friday night he hadn't been aware that she was no longer living at The Elms. Her divorce and remarriage had taken place while he was in jail, so it might have been Beryl whom he intended to see. But he hadn't. He'd seen no one at all. If Karl Morren was to be believed, he hadn't been near The Elms.

The thing was a jigsaw with half the pieces missing, yet, on the whole, I was prepared to swear that Beryl had somehow been at the bottom of things. Durford had once paid a surreptitious visit to The Elms, so why not Wayner? Then the very name Wayner recalled something else.

There was the day when I'd taken the photographs to The Carlo with the hope that someone might recognise Beryl Morren, as she then was, and so prove a connection between her and Wayner. As soon as I remembered that, I paid my bill and went on to the station. At the agency I took out the Morren file.

Because I rarely mention files you mustn't think they're not meticulously kept. When we're on a case everything done is fully reported and it's part of Bertha's job to type things out. Even I—and you might, I suppose, call me the boss of the concern—am subject to the same discipline; which was why I knew I'd find a full report of that visit to The Carlo. And I did.

It was a footnote that interested me. It went like this:

Why did Maria Carlo give that peculiar look when I said I was there enquiring about a woman associate of Wayner?

As I've said, I was ready to grasp at straws. That's why I was going to see Maria again. There'd been that queer look when I'd mentioned a woman, so maybe she'd been lying when she'd claimed that she'd never clapped eyes on Beryl Morren.

I hadn't the photographs of Beryl, but I did have the coloured original of Beryl standing with Greta. I put it in my pocket. It was well past my lunchtime and there was no point in going to The Carlo till the early afternoon, so I took my time over lunch at my usual pub. I even had a glass of port after it to give me time for a little more thinking.

If Maria had lied about Beryl Morren, then I'd be in a position to report to Jewle that I hadn't been far wrong after all when I'd suggested collusion between Beryl and Wayner in the matter of the diamonds. After that it ought to be up to him. I wouldn't go so far as to say I was a happy man as I paid my bill. I was definitely an optimistic one, which was more than I could have said about myself in the course of the last few days.

It was about half-past two when I got to The Carlo. I made almost instinctively for Harry's office and then I stopped. Mightn't it be better to short-circuit Harry? Mightn't Maria speak more freely if she knew that what she said was being treated as confidential?

A waiter came up to me just as I entered the restaurant.

"Sorry, sir. Lunches are over."

"I know," I said. "I just want a word with Maria. Is she about?"

He said I'd find her at the desk. She was going over the accounts, but she looked up when I coughed. I smiled down at her.

"How are you, Maria? You remember me? Travers?"

She remembered. Everyone does, as I said.

"You came about Dave Wayner," she said. "It's horrible what they say he's done."

"You still don't believe it?"

"Perhaps I do," she said. "All I know is, I wish I'd never seen him."

"He's a dangerous man," I said. "I know. But it was not about him that I wanted to see you. You remember a photograph you were given in your uncle's office to enquire about? The photograph of a woman. In case she'd ever been here. Would you mind having another look at it. It's not the same one, but it's pretty good. The one standing with her is her daughter."

She had a look. She stared. Her mouth gaped slightly.

"That's the one! The daughter. That's the one I saw Dave with."

I don't know just why, but her lip began to pucker and in a moment she was crying. A minute and she was herself again. Just a last dab at her eyes.

"I'm sorry," she said. "It brought things back: that was all."

She began to tell me about it. I think now she was glad to get it off her mind. She didn't remember dates, but it was the early summer before the Corby Street affair. She and Dave had been pretty close up till then. There'd been a cooling off and she'd seen him once or twice dancing with another woman. When she'd faced him with it, he'd said it was nothing at all. Then she'd seen the two together just by chance one afternoon in a Fuller's tea-shop in town. When she'd tried to be clever and had asked him if it was he she'd seen in town, he said he hadn't been anywhere near town that afternoon.

I had what I wanted. I didn't want to dot any i's, but before I could thank her and go she was asking who the woman actually was. It was best to lie. She and her mother, I said, had been on holiday from Kenya. They were back there now. I doubted if we'd ever clap eyes on either of them again.

Another five minutes and a train was taking me back to the City, but it wasn't too easy to think things out. When you've just been on what I might call the lucky end of a miracle, you've first got to be sure it really was a miracle before you can judge what luck it's actually going to bring. But a miracle it had certainly been. I'd set out that morning with only the vaguest of ideas and had ended with something that might solve the whole case.

Even before I was back at the agency I knew I had the answer to the strange conduct of Helen Cambon. It was just that Greta Sievers was scared to death about what had once happened between Greta Morren and David Wayner. She'd learned that he was being released and had been terrified he should try to get into touch. Helen had been asked to know nothing of her present where-abouts, no matter who enquired.

I settled down at my desk to try to work out the full implications of that liaison, over three years ago, between Greta Morren and Wayner. I'd hardly got down to it before I came up against something so startling that I had to lean back in the chair, wondering just what I should do. There seemed just one thing—to get hold of Jewle.

When I did get him, I told him something important had suddenly cropped up: something that concerned Wayner and the Durford murder as well as any interest I still might have in the Morren diamonds. It seemed to me so urgent that I ought to see him straight away.

I went to the Yard. He had offered to come to me, but that would have been out of his way. All I told him was what I'd happened to learn from Maria Carlo. I just wanted to see if it would have for him implications different from those it had had for me. The trouble was he hadn't been so near to the Morren side of things as we had. He was just trying to be interested till I told him about Helen Cambon.

"I think you should see her straight away," I said. "I don't know when she closes down, but it might be at five. Get her to tell you whether or not a man answering Wayner's description called there last Thursday afternoon. Everything depends on what she says."

We went by Underground: it was quicker. Jewle did all the talking. I was introduced as a colleague, which brought me none too pleasant a look. She was certainly loyal. She still denied knowledge of Greta's whereabouts.

"It's your choice," Jewle told her. "We could ask you to come to Scotland Yard and keep you there till we were satisfied you were telling the truth. Now we'll probably have to call you as a material witness, which'll mean giving evidence publicly under oath. So why not be reasonable? I give you my word that Mrs. Sievers will never know."

"Very well," she said. "Perhaps I *was* asked not to divulge the address."

"Thank you," Jewle said soberly. "Now just one more question. We have an idea there was an enquiry about the address as long ago as last Thursday. Probably in the afternoon. A man in, say, the early thirties. A rather pale complexion. Just above medium height."

"There was," she said. "I think it was when you said. He was very pleasant at first, but when I said I'd no idea where Greta was he was almost rude. He kept on insisting till I said I'd call the police if he didn't leave."

There was no missing the implication. I did some telephoning at the Tube station. I had Bernard's number, so I rang him.

"It's Travers again," I said. "I needn't ask if you're going to be in this evening?"

"Don't think I'll be stirring very far," he said. "Here to the kitchen, that's about all."

"Fine," I said. "I'll drop in and see you. Just a little surprise. In just over half an hour. That suit you?"

"Suits me fine," he said. "You won't tell me what it's all about?"

"If I did it wouldn't be a surprise."

I rang off. His guess would probably be that I'd ask him if he was fit enough to be taken out to dinner.

We didn't hurry; even then we were early in Flagon Street; the bookshop below the apartment was only just closing. We waited for another five minutes before mounting the stairs. It was I who rang the bell.

Bernard gave me a welcoming smile. Jewle suddenly appeared behind me and the smile went.

"Mind if I come in too?" Jewle said. "I shan't keep you long."

I kept my eyes away. I wondered what Bernard was thinking. Then courtesy got the upper hand.

"Of course. Superintendent. Do come in. Nothing serious has happened, I hope."

"Depends on how you look at it." Jewle said. "Not that I'm staying. Just wanted to ask you one question."

"Yes?"

"Why did you lie to us about that burglar?"

I'VE rarely seen a man so taken aback. He stammered something, but words just wouldn't come.

"It was David Wayner who came here," Jewle said. "There was no breaking in. You let him in. What he wanted you to tell him was where your sister was. She'd told you about her association with him over three years ago. Isn't that so?"

He shook his head.

"But it was nothing. Just a sort of brief acquaintance, that was all. She was afraid he might have taken it more seriously. Might make trouble between her and Frank. That's her husband, Frank Sievers."

"I know," Jewle said. "I almost owe you an apology. Mind if I take off my coat?

"You told your sister," he said, "that if Wayner did happen to see you you'd tell him nothing. Which you did. Under the circumstances, and considering what happened to you, that was pretty brave. It even partly excuses the lie. But it was wasted courage, Mr. Morren. There's only one person who can protect your sister, and that's herself."

Bernard looked puzzled.

"Her interests are still yours? You have a great affection for your sister?"

"Of course."

"What time does her husband get home of an evening?"

He glanced at his watch.

"Usually at about six."

"Right," Jewle said. "If you want to help your sister, this is what you're to do. Ring her at once. Say we've discovered who the burglar was. Say you think there may be a chance that Wayner knows she's living at Northwood. Make her get over here at once. Tell her to leave a message for her husband that you're not feeling too good."

He did the job well. What exactly the reactions were at the other end of the line we could pretty well judge. When he rang off he told us she'd be along as quickly as she could make it.

"Thank you," Jewle said. "You're not going to be sorry about this. Now would you mind making us all a cup of tea? Mr. Travers and I would like a minute or two to talk things over."

He waited till the kitchen door had closed behind Bernard. "So that's that," he went on. "I think Mrs. Sievers will talk. She'll realise that she's got to. The question is, what do we tell her?"

"There's Maria Carlo's evidence," I said. "Also that Greta once had Wayner meet her at The Elms. That ought to be enough."

"Yes," Jewle said. "But in the light of what we now know, you're pretty sure about Durford?"

I said I was. He had the reputation of being a good man on a trail, so he'd almost certainly followed Wayner that Thursday afternoon to Helen Cambon at Mayfair, and then again when he'd gone back to the hotel. He'd been on his heels when Wayner had gone to Flagon Street. He'd listened at the door, and when he'd thought Wayner was killing someone he nipped down to the callbox near-by and dialled 999.

He'd been lucky enough to get back on Wayner's trail when he emerged from the apartment, and had been close behind him at the hotel. He'd gone up to Wayner's room a minute or so later. He'd told Wayner who he was and what he'd seen and heard at the apartment. That was his way of putting on pressure. He'd got round to the diamonds, which was when Wayner had started to string him along.

"Yes," Jewle said. "I'm with you all the way. Wayner saw how to kill a couple of birds with one stone. He could get a car and he could see Karl Morren. Morren was his last chance for finding out where Greta was. In other words, Karl Morren told us quite a pack of lies."

That was how it looked. Jewle now thought, as I'd thought, that Wayner hadn't intended to kill Durford. After seeing Morren and learning where Greta was he'd have tried to see her. The rest we hadn't yet worked out.

"Put that young man out of his misery," Jewle told me. "Tell him to bring in that tea."

Bernard was all nerves. There was something I wanted to ask him. It might take his mind off the problem of his sister.

As soon as an opportunity occurred I put the question.

"Where did you live, Bernard, before you went to Cockfosters?"

He seemed to brighten up at once.

"At Calders End," he said. "It's quite a nice little place out Waltham Cross way."

"Handy for town?"

"Just a short walk to a main-line station. Quite near the country too. I liked it there."

"Your grandfather didn't live there too?"

He actually smiled.

"Oh no. Grandfather Morren was a town bird. Clerkenwell was good enough for him. He liked to be near the business."

The talk petered out to nothing in particular. Another half-hour went by and then I suddenly pricked my ears. There was definitely a sound on the stairs.

"We'll go in the other room," Jewle said quietly. "Soon as your sister's settled down we'll come in."

The bedroom door was slightly ajar. What Jewle must have been hoping for was some remark, or even confession, that would give him a lead.

No sooner was she in the room than she was asking questions.

"Bernard, what is it? Tell me the truth. How could anyone know David Wayner came here?"

"The police know," he said. "Come and sit down."

"Not till you tell me," she said. "How do they know?"

"I don't know. I think they know practically everything."

"Oh, my God! What am I going to do?"

Jewle opened the door. She stared as if he'd been a ghost.

I couldn't help staring too. Since I'd last seen her she'd aged ten years. Her face was pale: her eyes looked sunken and dark.

"Sorry to alarm you, Mrs. Sievers. Please sit down. And don't blame your brother. I practically forced him to get you to come here."

She sat down. The room was warm but she was shivering.

"That's better," Jewle said. "You were asking what you ought to do, so I'll tell you. First of all there's something you have to understand. We're here to help. You're in trouble, and because of David Wayner, but we can't help you if you don't tell us all about it."

"I can't," she said. "I can't. You don't want to help me. You couldn't help me."

"But we could," he told her patiently. "Listen, Mrs. Sievers. I've a daughter of about your age. I'm talking to you just as I would to her if I knew she was in trouble. So tell us all about it."

"I can't! I mean—I mean, I daren't."

Jewle smiled. "Because it might break up your home? You're here, talking to people who want to help you. Talking in confidence. You mustn't force me to go over all this in the presence of your husband. That's the alternative."

"No," she said. "Not that. I'll tell you. I'll tell you everything."

"I'm glad." he said. "Believe me, it's the only wise thing to do. Take your time. We're in no hurry. Begin with when you first met David Wayner."

She didn't have to think for more than a moment or two.

"It was at a place called The Carlo," she said. "I went there with the Yarrows. You remember, Bernard. It was George Yarrow's birthday or something and they were throwing a party, and after dinner we danced. That's where I met him. I suppose you could say I fell for him. I met him there again, and then he didn't want me to go there any more and we met once or twice in town. Then one day he asked if I could borrow a car: he knew I hadn't one of my own, and I said I could: my mother's little car before she bought the Jaguar. He said he wanted to show me his old home.

"So I got Mother to let me have the car and I met him at New Barnet and we went to a place called Insbury. He showed me the Hall and then he said he was going to play a joke on an old friend. We went back to the village and I was to keep the car engine ticking over in case this friend should find out and we had to get away fast."

"I know," Jewle said. "That was the Insbury bank robbery. And you found out about it."

"Yes," she said. "I read about it in the papers, so I rang him and said I was going to report it to the police. He just laughed. 'Oh no, you're not,' he said. 'We were in it together. You were the one who found the car and helped us get away.'

"So what could I do? I said I never wanted to see him again and if he pestered me I really would tell the police. And that was all that happened till the November and then he rang me. He said he had to have five hundred pounds. He said he was desperate and if he didn't get it he was going to the police and I'd be incriminated too."

"So it was you who took that two hundred pounds," I said.

"No," she told me quickly. "I wouldn't do that. I sent him my key to the breakfast-room and I made a mould for the safe key with some Plasticene. I told him how to get to the house and where the safe was." She shook her head. "I suppose I did take it really."

"Don't think that," Jewle said. "You were under pressure. You were being blackmailed. And what happened then?"

She thought for a moment or two.

"I thought everything was going to be all right. I'd met Frank—my husband—and I was really beginning to forget all about David Wayner, and then he rang me again. It was in the January. He said he had to have some more money."

I thought for a moment she was going to cry, but she didn't.

"I was absolutely desperate. I even thought of running away somewhere. And then I thought of this scheme. It was when I knew Uncle Lorenz was coming over and bringing Daddy some diamonds. So I told him about it, and what the safe combination was and how he could get the door key—"

"Just a minute," Jewle said. "How'd you know about that?"

Bernard chipped in. "The key was always in the door in the daytime. We used to go there sometimes when there was anything special to see, just before it was sent away."

"I see. So you did all that, Mrs. Sievers. And then?"

"You don't understand," she said. "I wanted him to be caught. That's why I warned the police. I told him not to do anything till a quarter-past six and I rang the police from here while Bernard was finishing dressing."

"I just can't believe it!" That was Bernard.

"Don't be a hypocrite," Jewle told him sharply. "How do you know what you'd have done under the same circumstances? So you did what you did, Mrs. Sievers, and Wayner was caught. Didn't you anticipate any trouble for yourself?"

"I just didn't care any more," she said. "It was a kind of gamble. If he brought me into it, then I was going to tell the police everything. I couldn't go on as I was."

"In some ways you did a public service," he said. "You hoped Wayner would be away for a very long time?"

"The train robbers got thirty years. I didn't think he'd get as long as that. By the time he came out I thought everything would be better. I had no one to talk to. I just had to do everything myself."

"I know," he said. "But things didn't work out quite that way. All he got was four years and he didn't serve even that. And what did you think would happen when he came out?"

"I thought he'd kill me. That's why I asked Helen not to know where I was. When she rang me and said he'd been in I was terrified, and then when he came here and attacked Bernard I just didn't know what to do. It was a nightmare. And then I read about how he'd killed a man."

Her lip puckered and this time she really did cry. It was as if the whole of that small room was part of the tragedy.

Jewle waited for a moment.

"Don't worry about Wayner, Mrs. Sievers. We'll take care of him. No one will know it, but you'll be looked after from now on. He'll be caught long before he comes anywhere near you. Perhaps I could use your phone, Mr. Morren."

The sobbing had ceased by the time he'd finished.

"What're you going to do with me?"

Jewle smiled. "Do with you? Nothing at all. You're going home to your husband and daughter. You'll say your brother wasn't so ill that he couldn't look after himself. So if you'd like to go and powder your nose we'll see about getting you back."

She disappeared through the bedroom door. Jewle turned to Bernard. He wasn't smiling.

"Just a word of warning, Mr. Morren. Nothing's to be mentioned about all this. You understand? Not to a living soul, even your father. You're far from in the clear your-self: don't forget that. You lied to us. You made fools of us this afternoon when you pretended to try to identify the man who'd attacked you. Scotland Yard doesn't like being made a fool of; so, as I said, it depends on you. Keep your mouth shut and we may drop charges. Understood?"

He understood.

We'd had to wait a minute or two till the car arrived. Jewle took over the driving seat and Greta sat with him in front. I shared the back with one of Jewle's sergeants and a constable. It was a longish drive, and when we got to Northwood itself Greta had to tell Jewle the way. We went through the town, then sharp left towards the golf-course. At the entry to the actual road Jewle stopped the car. There was only a hundred yards now for Greta to walk.

The men were given instructions. I sat in front with Jewle when we set off back.

"Where to now?" I said.

"It's been a long day," he said. "I feel like getting a meal before thinking all this over. A scratch meal at the Yard suit you too?"

I rang Bernice from a callbox in the town. It was well after eight o'clock when we got to the Yard. Coffee and sandwiches came in and then we began to talk.

It was only in the quiet of that room that what we'd learned could really dawn on us. All we'd had to start with had been that Greta Morren had once been friendly with Wayner and that after his term of imprisonment she was desperately anxious to avoid him. All the rest had come clean out of the blue.

"What about her?" I said.

"Don't know. It's been worrying me. After all, but for her that diamond robbery would never have taken place. Frankly, I wouldn't know how to frame a charge. I think I'll sit on it for a day or two."

"The diamonds," I said. "How does what she told us affect the diamonds?"

"It doesn't," he said. "We still don't know whether Wayner decided to do that job on his own or whether he preferred to have a confederate."

I didn't agree. Wayner, I was beginning to think, was the lone-wolf type. And he'd had that Corby Street job handed to him on a silver platter, so why bring in a confederate to share the loot?

"You realise what you're suggesting?"

I didn't, till he pointed it out.

"When Wayner was trapped he didn't have those diamonds on him. That's not even arguable. He just didn't. Also they weren't concealed anywhere on the premises or thrown over the back wall. The door key was thrown over the wall. We did find that, but no diamonds. That leaves only one answer. The diamonds were never in the safe."

"But Lorenz Brander saw Morren put them in! And Morren didn't go upstairs again once he'd come down."

Jewle got up.

"Look," he said. "I'm Morren and you're Brander. You're just over there at the table. When I open the safe I'm between you and it. I say, 'Better put these away for the night', and I do so. Then I change my mind but I don't say so. Absent-mindedness? I don't know. I slip the diamonds into my pocket instead, because they'll be just as safe. You're not watching me. Why should you be? So, according to Brander, the diamonds were put in the safe."

"You're implying that Morren put them in his pocket in—well, in good faith?"

"Of course! How could he know there was going to be a robbery? In the morning he was going to take them to the bank or else to the workshop. Depended on what he was actually making. Then he was called up by us early the next morning and told there'd been a burglary and the safe had been opened. Now do you see?"

If things had been as he'd said, I did. It had been a heaven-sent chance to make ten thousand pounds.

"I think you're right," I said. "Morren needed money. He had heavy commitments and there was that settlement with his wife. Let alone his lady friend elsewhere. So what do we do? We can't prove a thing."

"We'll sleep on it," Jewle said. "It isn't Morren that's worrying me at the moment—it's Wayner. We want him, and badly. And when you think about Wayner, ask yourself a question. Is it because he's dead that we can't find him?"

He held up a hand.

"No, don't answer. Just add something else when you're doing the thinking. You can bury a body, but how're you going to bury a car?"

15. OAK AND ACORN

JEWLE rang me at the flat while I was having breakfast. One or two things had turned up—a Commander's conference for one—so would I put off our meeting till the afternoon.

"I have a vague idea I owe you a lunch," he said, "so what about the usual place at one o'clock. The slate ought to be clean by then."

I'd done quite a lot of thinking since I'd left him the previous night. One thing I thought was that he might have told me more, or was I being unreasonable? He was after Wayner for the killing of Durford, which was no real concern of mine. My only reasons for asking Jewle's help had been in the exceedingly vague matter of the whereabouts of some stolen diamonds. While he was always willing to stretch a point, there'd been no real reason why he should have kept me informed as to how the hunt for Wayner had been getting along.

All the same, if I could read aright that final cryptic remark of his the previous night, then the Yard's conclusion now was that Wayner was dead. And if so, it was highly probable that Karl Morren had killed him, and on the Friday night. Now that we knew the real story of the Corby Street robbery we had a really definite reason why Wayner should have been making for The Elms from the moment he left the Sanford Hotel in Durford's car. Not only would he want to know the whereabouts of Morren's daughter, he'd also want to hear from Morren just how much truth there'd been in the story Greta had told him.

That was as far as I could move with any certainty. Once Wayner was inside the house he'd have been operating at the right end of a gun—the gun that had killed Durford. How, then, could Morren have killed him? Even without a gun. Wayner could have smashed Morren in a couple of seconds, and, from what he had done to Bernard Morren and Durford. he'd been in a savage mood.

So there I was: unable—and probably like Jewle—to prove with any certainty that Wayner was dead. But if he *were* dead, then proof might lie in the finding of Durford's car. As Jewle had said, you can hide a body, but where, in these days, are you going to hide a car? Even if Wayner had managed to slip abroad, he couldn't have taken the car with him. Too much red-tape is needed for that, and Wayner had had no time. Also that car had been highly publicized. Every police force and car dealer and motoring association knew the make, colour and registration number.

That thinking had been done the previous night. As soon as I was awake the next morning I'd taken up where I'd left off, and this time I began working on the assumption that Karl Morren *had* killed Wayner at The Elms. At once the body would have had to be disposed of, and the logical thing to do would have been to take it somewhere in Wayner's own car.

Mind you, I had to slur over some difficulties: how, for instance, a man like Morren could have got Wayner's body from the house and out to the road where the car must have been parked. One thing, however, was a certainty. Morren couldn't have moved the body in his own car. That would have left Wayner's car still to be disposed of.

Very well then, I said to myself. Somehow Morren got Wayner's body in the car and then drove off. The servants were in their flat and probably watching television. They'd have heard nothing. Even if they had heard a car, it would have been nothing unusual. Plenty of cars must have used that road. So Morren drove quietly off. Where to? I didn't know the district too well, but in a district of few, if any, secluded spots, in an almost completely built-up area, he could hardly have hidden the body locally. And there was always the problem of the car. It would have been found far too near The Elms.

And that was how I suddenly thought of Morren's old home at Calders End. I got out a large-scale map of the northern suburbs and found the place, and what surprised me at once was the comparative nearness to Cockfosters. I'd been thinking of distances like fifteen or even twenty miles, but as soon as I measured it it was only eight. Eight miles, I said to myself. Morren could have hidden car and body there and then have walked back. Or he could have picked up a late bus near Enfield and shortened the journey by at least an hour.

I collected my car and set off. To do the job thoroughly I had to start from near Cockfosters and take from there the route that Morren would have taken. I was fairly early. By ten o'clock I was taking a quiet road that skirted Enfield before bringing me back on the A. 105. Then I went slightly wrong. In busy suburban traffic you've no time to see directions. England's, in any case, the most badly posted place in Europe, which was why I trusted to my sense of direction and took the easy left-hand fork instead of the right. After a couple of miles I realised I was making for, of all places, Potters Bar, so I slowed down at the next direction indicators. I hadn't gone too badly wrong. A sharp right-hand turn took me into a comparatively quiet road just three miles from Calders End.

Mind you, I might have discovered what I did if I'd come into the place from the right direction. And I might not. At any rate, I was about a quarter of a mile away, and still on that quiet road, when I noticed the mounds away to my left. I slowed the car down till I came to a kind of track. By the side of it was a wooden notice:

PRIVATE PROPERTY
TRESPASSERS WILL BE PROSECUTED

I drew the car in on the verge and got out. The track was overgrown and in places shrubs were overhanging it. A few yards and it began to mount. It went round to the right, still rising, then made a steepish descent, and then I saw what the whole place had once been—a gravel-pit. To my right was a hill from the base of which gravel had once been excavated.

To the left of the workings was a small lake of about half an acre, nestling, as it were, under the cliff.

I went back to the car and drove slowly on. Round the bend came the first of the bungalows and then the beginnings of a street. There was a school and, just beyond it, a sweetshop. An old-fashioned bell tinkled as I went in, and an elderly man appeared. I asked if he was on the telephone. He wasn't.

"You lived here long?" I said.

"Most of my life," he said.

"Then you can tell me about those old gravel workings up the road. How long have they been derelict?"

"Must be about ten years," he said. "That road used to be wired off, but you know what kids are these days. They soon had it down. Skating and sliding mostly: that's about the only time they go there nowadays."

I went on to the post-office and used the callbox to phone the Yard. There was just the hope that Jewle mightn't yet be in conference, and he wasn't. I told him what I'd found. It was a long shot and no more, but I'd thought I ought to report.

It was an hour before a sergeant of his arrived. He was a youngish man named Trumper: smart as they come, and they come pretty smart these days. We used his car to go along to those old workings.

We had a good look at the track. Here and there were definite marks of tyres.

"The trouble is there was a sharpish frost that Friday night," he said. "Moonlight too. That would have made it possible to get along here without lights, especially if he knew the lie of the land."

We went on up to the top of the rise. There'd once been protective railings there, but now they were badly gapped.

"This might be the spot," he said. "All he'd have to do was start from here, put the car in neutral and give it a push."

He went carefully forward, got down on his stomach and looked over the edge.

"Not all that much drop. Wonder how deep the water is?"

I'd wondered that too, which was why I'd seen the man at the sweet-shop again. He'd reckoned it might be at least twelve feet.

"Deep enough to hide a car, if there's one there," I said. "So what do we do now?"

He said he'd have to get back to the Yard. If Jewle thought it worth while, he'd probably be back himself that afternoon with a couple of frogmen. If a car was there, it could be salvaged later. All that would be immediately needed was a rough identification of the car and getting out the body.

We parted company at the post-office. I took the direct route back to town, and it was just about lunchtime when I got to the agency. I didn't know what to do about Jewle, so I just stayed put in case he should ring me. He didn't. I had a sandwich lunch in my office and nobody rang. I hung about on tenterhooks all the afternoon, and still nobody rang. Bertha brought in tea just after four o'clock, and it was not long after that when Jewle at last came on the line.

"Jewle," he said. "Ringing from Calders End. You were dead right. Ten minutes ago they brought up Wayner's body."

"A lucky break," I said. "And what now?"

"You and I are going to see Morren," he said. "I'd like it to be at roughly about the time when Wayner could have seen him on Friday night. Say just after nine. I'll pick you up at the flat just after eight. That all right with you?"

I told him it certainly was.

It was just short of nine o'clock when Jewle drew the car in at the kerb. It was much as it had been before: no sign of light above the garage but a faint light coming through the fanlight of the front door. During the minute or so that we sat there a couple of cars went by. The road was none too well lighted and it would be quite a time before the moon rose. Jewle said everything was to be as arranged. He'd do the talking. Morren would incriminate himself.

It was Morren who opened the door. We couldn't see his face and he didn't switch on the drive light.

"May we come in?" Jewle said.

Morren drew back.

"Of course," he said. "You wanted to see me about something?"

We went into the lounge. The television was still on, but he turned it off.

"Do sit down, gentlemen. You'd like a drink?"

He looked perfectly composed. Jewle said we wouldn't be staying all that long.

"What we're here for, Mr. Morren, is about you yourself," he said, "so I'll come straight to the point. We have irrefutable evidence that you lied to us about David Wayner being here last Friday night. He *was* here. So suppose you tell us all about it."

Morren thought for a moment. "Very well. Superintendent. He was here. I didn't want any scandal, so I lied."

"So far, so good. Now tell us what happened. Every word that was said."

Morren shrugged his shoulders. "Nothing was said. I mean, nothing of any importance. For some reason or other he wanted my daughter's address. He said he'd known her before he went to jail and she had still some property of his he wanted to recover. I thought it was fishy, so I gave him a fictitious address. And that's the last I saw of him."

"Oh no," Jewle said. "That wasn't the last you saw of him. It isn't even remotely like what happened. And don't try to look indignant. Wayner's body was recovered this afternoon from the pond at those old gravel workings where you dropped it, and the car, last Friday night."

He didn't crumple up. For a moment he looked stunned. The colour seemed to leave his face. He buried his face in his hands.

"Tell us about it," Jewle said. "Get it off your mind."

A minute and he was looking up.

"Very well," he said. "I'll tell you."

"Just one moment," Jewle said. "Let me tell you something else first. We know that Wayner didn't rob you of any diamonds. Don't ask us how we know, but we know."

"I didn't mean to take them. I don't know quite how it was, but I put them in my pocket. I thought I'd take them to the bank in the morning after all. Then the robbery happened and—well, I wanted the money."

"Right. Now tell us what happened that Friday night."

I'll tell it to you in my own words. Morren's account was disjointed. Every now and again he'd go off the track and have to be led back to it.

There'd been a knock at the door. Wayner was there and he'd pushed past Morren and gone into the lounge. Morren hadn't recognised him, but before he could speak Wayner had introduced himself. Morren had told him to get out or he'd call the police. That was when Wayner produced a gun.

He told Morren precisely why he wanted to see Greta. Still with the gun pointing at Morren, he wanted to know what had happened to the diamonds. Morren had been staggered at what he'd learned about Greta.

"I had to do something," he said. "If it was true. I had to try and protect her."

"And yourself," Jewle said. "If the truth came out about the diamonds you were a ruined man. But carry on. Tell us what you did."

Morren told Wayner to put away the gun. There was no need for any compulsion.

"I want to get to the bottom of this as much as you do," he'd said. "We'll go and see my daughter. She's living only a mile or so away."

He left the cloakroom door open while he got his hat and coat, but he managed to pocket his own gun. He'd expected trouble and he'd bought a gun just before Wayner had been released. He and Wayner went to the car, and Morren didn't turn on the drive light.

He gave directions while Wayner drove. At a secluded spot about half a mile beyond the station he told Wayner to slow down.

"Then I shot him," he said. "I stopped the car and got out and pushed his body down below the window. Then I drove on to Calders End."

"Yes," Jewle said. "I think that's about how it happened. We found that Webley of his in his pocket when he was fished up this afternoon."

"The diamonds," I said. "What actually happened to them?"

He didn't answer for a moment. He seemed to be thinking back.

"The diamonds?"

"Yes," I said. "What happened to them? Did you use them? Sell them, or what?"

"No," he said. "I still have them. They're in my study. You'd like me to fetch them?"

Everything happened as quickly as I can tell it. He got slowly to his feet and made for the door to the right of the fireplace. He went through and left it open, though all we could see was the wall immediately inside. Then there was the shot!

He was lying on the floor, just in front of his desk. The right temple was uppermost and you'd only to look at it to know he was dead.

Even the sound of that shot hadn't been heard from the flat above the garage. Jewle did some telephoning while I looked through the drawers of that desk in case the diamonds should really be there. But they weren't. It had been folly even to look for them. They'd been only a subterfuge once Morren had known just what he had to do.

The ambulance came. The servants appeared. Jewle told them Mr. Morren had been suddenly taken ill and they'd better get back to their flat once they let us out. It was about ten o'clock when we went out to the car.

We sat there for a minute or two. It was as if we wanted to review alone the far too sudden happenings of that night.

"Like an oak tree coming out of an acorn," Jewle said. "If Greta Sievers had never gone to The Carlo none of this would have happened. Now three people are dead."

"What about her?"

"She won't have to worry about Wayner," he said. "I rang her earlier and told her he was dead. She couldn't say anything. I think she was crying."

"And what's going to be done about her? You think you ought to bring a case?"

I think I've said before that Jewle has an infinite capacity for surprising me. He was to do it again.

"Funny you should ask that," he said. "You're pretty well acquainted with *A Midsummer Night's Dream*?"

"I think so," I said. "Why?"

"Well, there's a line towards the end which I've often had to think of in my line of business. It's after the rustics have finished their play and Theseus says, '*When the players are all dead, there's none to be blamed.*' That's how it is now. Or don't you agree?"

"I'm not cut out to be a judge," I told him. "All I know is it'll be a long time before she sleeps very sound."

He said we'd better be getting along. At the side road he reversed the car. I hoped he wouldn't be passing the spot where Durford had been killed. I, too, would have some not too pleasant thoughts.

Jewle didn't go that way. At the fork he turned left.

"You might be lucky after all," he told me. "Morren virtually robbed United Assurance of ten thousand pounds. Couldn't it be recovered from his estate?"

I said it might. I don't think I said it with any enthusiasm. Somehow, after what had happened that night, it didn't seem to matter.

THE END